I was once on a flight in Africa

I was once on a flight in Africa

ESBJÖRN SÖDERMARK

I was once on a flight in Africa

© Esbjörn Södermark 2022

Förlag: BoD – Books on Demand, Stockholm, Sverige

Tryck: BoD – Books on Demand, Norderstedt, Tyskland

ISBN: 978-91-8057-038-1

Prologue

I was once on a flight in Africa. That's where it all happened.

It definitely affected me. I think it may even have changed me to some extent. For the better, I hope. At least it must have helped me grow as a person in some way, like problems, trouble and hardship often do – if we allow them to.

I can walk you through it, if you would care to let me do that.

I can definitely say that if events had not unfolded in the way they did, I would not be around to tell the story – and that is the story of what actually happened on flight AFRA314 from Maputo, Mozambique with destination Windhoek, Namibia.

Had I known before I went on this trip what I was about to encounter on that flight, I would never have left home. And then I would have missed out on what would become an adventure of a lifetime. I'm such a coward! Good thing that I didn't know.

Chapter 1

Please, allow me to make a boring introduction of myself. My name is Karl Sandström. I'm a Swedish citizen, and a recently retired accountant. I was born and raised in the north of Sweden but nowadays I live in a small town in the south.

My physical appearance is (apart from being terribly old) rather tall, almost no hair, a trimmed beard which does its job to cover things up and a waistline replaced by unnecessary extra weight. In short, an old man whose appearance is marked by too little sleep, too little exercise, too much food and a fair amount of stress.

My life up to this point has rendered me four children and a broken marriage. The children have their own families and they all live far away from me. I see them from time to time, though, but not too often. They call me when they need me, which is beginning to be less and less frequent. It's been said that parents have the task of giving their children two things; roots and wings. I think perhaps I've been successful in giving them wings. At least the wings have been successful in carrying the children away.

But it's good to know that they manage. That is how I choose to interpret the fact that I don't hear from them too often. I must have done something right in my parenting, if they manage life without too much help from me.

Not long ago I moved to a new apartment in the town where I live. I must say, I enjoy my new apartment very much. It's a nice apartment in a nice part of a nice town. Perfect for my needs, and much to my liking. After being properly installed and set, I noticed that I began being inflicted with some sort of sad boredom, almost resembling a mild depression. I realised that I was really lucky, and that I really had everything, and that I really had absolutely nothing to look forward to, and that I really struggled to find a reason to get up in the morning. This is a wonderful spot, I thought to myself, in which I can sit and slowly wither away until the day when also my withering days have withered away.

I became acutely aware of the fact that my career had ended, and no one needed me anymore, and that I had nothing to make me excited about the future. Also, as I mentioned; my children had all since long moved out, and they now have families and lives of their own.

Luckily, at least I didn't feel sorry for myself. Definitely not... Ah, who am I kidding? Of course, I felt sorry for myself. Heaps! My pool of self-pity was frequently in use, not only because of the fact that the edges around it are slippery and sloping... Besides, there was not much else to occupy one's time with.

So, I lead a quiet life in my apartment. It is actually quiet to the extent that I regularly find myself talking to myself on various subjects. Sometimes the subjects are simple, such as what to wear outside today or how to best open a jar. But from time to time, I engage in lengthy and/or heated discussions with myself – which I always win, I might add. That's just one way of boosting one's self confidence, although at the same time one's self esteem takes a hit from the fact that the only way to achieve the win is to have the fight with oneself and thereby beat oneself up in the process. All a bit sad really.

One thing which is good for body and mind is taking walks. I try to take walks, if not every day, at least every other day. It's just that I find walking so terribly boring. I need a goal and a reason for walking. Walking for its own sake just doesn't do it for me. To motivate myself I try to find a reason for the walk, which most often is just going to the store to buy groceries or other necessities. The problem, as I see it, with walking in the neighbourhood where you live, is that however hard you try to make it different each time, you still leave from the front door just to return to the same front door a while later. One day you start the walk to the left and the next day to the right, but after a couple of times you've seen everything there is to see in walking distance of your home.

During one of my boring walks, I was passing through town. There I ran into an old acquaintance. I can't say we're close but he looked happy to see me and I was happy enough to see him, so I said "Hi! How are you?" And he said "Yeah well, you know…" (This was not the kind of situation in which to say. "No, I don't. That's why I asked.")

"What about you?" He asked. "Yeah, yeah." I answered.

That concluded the greeting ceremony and it was time to tackle more important topics like… ahm… like… ahm… like the weather! (Always a safe conversational rescue in Sweden.) "So, the weather could be better or what do you think? Still, it is what it is, right?" I started off strong. "Yes, that's true. I've seen worse, though. Do you remember last winter?" he asked. Yes, I do remember last winter. I just don't remember the weather. But then again, my life and the weather were as bleak then as they are now so it was no stretch to imagine it, even though I had no recollection of any specifics. "Yes, last winter… Yes, that was really…", I said, trying to make it sound convincing that I actually did remember the weather of last winter.

Anyway, with that said, the possible conversational topics were exhausted as was my conversational endurance and we said goodbye in the form of: "Good talking to you! Bye!" "Yes, bye!"

After this exciting event, I went home to enjoy some well-earned rest.

Yes, I lead a boring life. Fortunately, I haven't developed any obsessive compulsory disorder habits, aka OCD habits, at all. None whatsoever. I find it perfectly normal to empty the vacuum cleaner on the first day of each month, just to see and visually inspect how much dust has been sucked up the previous month. To buy eggs only in cartons containing 15 eggs is both practical and aesthetically appealing. Everyone knows that if you have an egg carton in your fridge and you keep picking the eggs closest to you when you remove eggs from the box, the centre of gravity will move farther and farther to the other side of the box and you will end up with the risk of dropping the box, and thereby causing you to engage in serious cleaning activities as an undesirable consequence. Who wants that? Also very important is the aesthetical aspect, and cartons with fifteen eggs in three rows of five, are the only ones where you can remove even or odd numbers of eggs and still be able to create a symmetrical pattern inside the box that will be aesthetically pleasing when you next time open the box.

Someone once made a remark about avoiding the entire weight distribution problem by just taking eggs from the far side of the box and not the closest side, but honestly, you don't have to listen to everyone.

There are possibly a couple of other minor issues, but nothing actually worth mentioning here. All of which I can totally defend, I might add.

As entertainment, or rather pastime, I've found YouTube invaluable. You can find almost everything on YouTube and spend hours and hours watching clips which YouTube decides to recommend to you. The video clips popping up are for the most part really interesting, persuading you to not turn the computer off, and thereby preventing you from going to sleep. Then again, perhaps not the best pastime for someone who has trouble sleeping, after all…

The YouTube channels which interest me the most are channels with real pilots talking and showing clips about everything that has to do with aviation. I find investigations of accidents and incidents especially interesting. I enjoy following expert investigations, which sometimes take years, in their relentless pursuit of the answer to the question "What went wrong and why?"

My son-in-law is a pilot, working for a major airline. He has provided me with every season of National Geographic's "Air Crash Investigation". I have seen every episode at least twice, and some episodes four, five times. Whenever

I'm about to go on a trip which involves flying, I always try to find the time to watch one or two episodes of "Air crash Investigation". I like to think that I'm prepared for every eventuality. I'm not, of course, but I like to think that I am.

It's been said that "time flies when you're having fun". Well, my time didn't fly. It dragged along slowly like an old retiree moving on tired legs on an uphill path. I knew for a fact that my path led me and my life downhill, but that didn't seem to help the time becoming airborne. Another breakfast, another day. Another dinner, another Netflix- or YouTube-evening, another sleepless night. Rinse and repeat.

I knew I had to do something. Maybe pick up a hobby, any hobby. How about stamp collecting? This must be exciting and exotic since no one nowadays uses stamps for sending mail with the post. I shivered. No, the excitement a latent philatelist should feel at this prospect refused to present itself. What else is there? Days went by and the weather in February in the south of Sweden also did a good job of keeping my spirit firmly on a low level.

Then it dawned on me; perhaps a little trip to a part of the world where the climate was more inductive to spirit-lifting. Where could that be? Thailand? No, if I really wanted to get away and experience new things, a country where half of Sweden's population was hiding from the weather at home was not it. Why not Africa? I've not seen much of Africa and somehow the prospect of exploring Africa on my own seemed intriguing.

Africa is of course a vast continent and where would I go? I thought about it long and hard, allowing the idea to mature into something almost resembling a decision. Did I know someone somewhere in Africa who could perhaps introduce me to the continent?

I then remembered that last year, on my birthday, I received a text message saying "Best birthday wishes from Nils in Africa". I also remember thinking "I don't know any Nils and I don't know anyone in Africa". This was truly a startling mystery. Who in the world could that be?! (Or rather, who in Africa could that be?!) This really bothered me. It could of course be a mistake, a message meant for somebody else, but it was undeniably my birthday and something about the name and Africa resonated with me.

From some dark and almost never used corner of my brain, a memory asked for my attention. At a reunion with mates from my old high school someone had said something about a guy from school who had moved to, and now lived in, Africa. His name was (and apparently still is) Nils. The intriguing question was of course, how did he know which date my birthday was (and actually still is)? We have had no contact since I left school, more than 45 years ago.

I answered his message and learned that it really was the Nils that I knew in high school. Apparently, he was now living in Mozambique. The explanation to why he managed to congratulate me on my actual birthday was that he had signed up at some internet site or other which specialised in letting school mates keep in touch. This website had old registers of classes in different schools with birth dates and such. The website then brought to his attention that this particular day was my birthday. He then just searched the internet for my phone number.

Imagine that! Internet… Who would have thought?

This was now my only lead to Africa and I decided to give it a go. First, I wanted to know where exactly in Mozambique he had settled down. I sent him a text in order to find out. The answer was Maputo, the capital. Next question: If I pop by, is there chance of getting a cup of coffee? The answer was yes, together with the reassuring message that I was very welcome to visit. That settled it. I was going to Africa! Preparations could start.

Visa application with photograph and my passport sent to the Mozambique Embassy in Stockholm. Supplementary vaccinations and prescription for malaria medication acquired. Passport and approved visa returned from the Embassy. Prescribed malaria pills purchased. Search for plane tickets initiated.

There are a number of possibilities to get from Sweden to Mozambique. One can take off from either Stockholm, Gothenburg or Copenhagen, then go via London and Johannesburg or via Frankfurt and Addis Ababa or via Geneva and Addis Ababa or via Amsterdam and Addis Ababa or via Brussels and Addis Ababa or just with one short stop in Paris, in Dubai or in Doha. I chose to buy a ticket for a flight from Stockholm to Maputo with a short stop in Doha, Qatar. More comfort, fewer stops, quicker, and less risk of having the checked in luggage being lost.

Planning was an essential part in my previous occupation as an accountant. In order to be able to keep deadlines e.g., a thorough planning was of utmost importance. The plans had to be well grounded in a correctly evaluated environment and contain adequate safety margins. It was not an option to declare to the employer or to the authorities;

"Sorry, I didn't make it. But, let's forget about now. Let's look forward, and hope that I'll be able to do better next year!" No, if I wanted to keep my job, I had to deliver quality, on time, every time.

Perhaps that is why I've found myself planning every move in my own home. Or is this perhaps just a consequence of who I am? Nevertheless, a journey between two rooms in my apartment entails a planning phase which begins with scanning the room in which the journey starts, identifying every object that possibly could be regarded as being misplaced. If such an object is identified, the planning process continues with establishing where this object rightfully belongs. Is that a room which I would pass when moving from room A to room B? Would it be necessary to move the object now or could it possibly wait until next time such a trip would be made?

It may sound like my apartment is huge. It's not. Sizewise it could better be described as small. So, it's not the apartment that is big. It's the planning process that is disproportionally extensive. The same planning process would be initiated even when moving around in the same room, e. g. the kitchen. Moving between the stove and the refrigerator involves a certain amount of planning, containing questions like; "what goes where, when and why?"

On the other hand, when I leave home for a journey I like to relax and leave as much as possible of worries and planning at home. Over time I've become more and more inclined to avoid unnecessary planning when I go on a trip. Previously I always bought return tickets and planned the whole trip before leaving home. This time I thought it would be more interesting to just buy the first ticket and then decide step by step where to go next and where to eventually end up.

A certain amount of preparation was inescapable, however. I was about to leave the latter part of winter in Sweden for the latter part of summer in Africa. This required a bit of preparation in the form of e. g. buying clothes suitable for an expedition such as this. Therefore, I bought myself a pair of khaki-coloured cargo-trousers and a couple of shirts in matching colours. I decided that this would have to do, since it could fit with what I already could find in my closet.

Along with the idea of exploring Africa perhaps in the hope of finding more favourable weather, or just for the sake of it, came a thought of possibly finding an alternative residence there. This thought was under development and perhaps not entirely serious at this point, but still, something worth considering. Maybe, and why not? I was looking for a change. Why not a more permanent one? I kept this thought as something to have in mind and to consider during my trip. Nothing much tied me to Sweden. Especially in this day and age geographical location holds less and less importance. Much of my social interactions were already on the telephone and over the internet, which made my actual location more or less irrelevant. Furthermore, much of Africa was in the same time zone as Sweden, which meant that there would be no need for anyone to interrupt their sleep at night in order to have a telephone conversation with me.

Arguments kept stacking up, and I felt more and more intrigued, more and more into the idea. It could of course also be because I did a good job of talking myself into it. This was even before I started my trip to Africa. I had no idea of what awaited me there, and yet, I was soon convinced of all the advantages of permanently living there.

Perhaps some of my friends and family members might argue against it, but in the end, they would understand. (Or simply be forced to accept it…) I kept thinking; Why not find a place to live which would be a bit more exciting than small-town Sweden? Maybe this could actually turn out to be the change I subconsciously was looking for? I wanted to find that out, and I wanted to continue considering it a possibility.

I realised, of course, that one of the more fundamental realities of moving from point A to point B is that one has to leave point A. Was I really ready to leave the comforting familiarity of the place I knew, in exchange for the scary, but exciting unknown? This was a question which, at least at a later stage, needed serious consideration.

Anyway, for the moment, I pushed all hesitation aside. This was exciting! Africa, here I come!

Chapter 2

My father used to say; "The only thing you need to bring on a trip is passport, tickets and money. Everything else you would need you can buy later." This was a long time ago but it is still true, with a couple of exceptions; you still need a valid passport but instead of tickets and money you need a smartphone and a credit card. Sometimes you actually need tickets on paper, but often a ticket in your smartphone is quite sufficient. In fact, sometimes the ticket it simply tied to your passport number, thus making it possible to check in for the flight only by showing your passport.

Having checked that I had passport with the visa, ticket, credit card and smartphone also with ticket in an app, and that I also packed "everything else I would need", I locked the door and went down the stairs to the taxi waiting in front of the house.

Halfway to the railway station I suddenly realised that there may have been a little flaw in what my father used to say. He never had the opportunity to go to Africa, which meant that malaria medication was never mentioned as a travel necessity by him. My malaria pills were still in my apartment, and I was in a taxi on my way to the railway station to catch a train that would take me to the airport. This was a splendid opportunity to panic – an opportunity I did not fail to use. The only way to get malaria pills is to have a prescription from a medical doctor. My prescription, even though computerised and accessible in a pharmacy at the airport, was used up and subsequently useless. The malaria pills I needed were lying on the kitchen table in the apartment I had left, and for every second became farther and farther away.

The instruction for the use of these particular malaria pills was that one should start taking the pills one or two days prior to entering malaria infested area. I did. I'm an accountant. I live for following instructions. It's just that I forgot to put the box of pills back in its designated place in the luggage.

It didn't help that I knew exactly why I had taken them out of the luggage and placed them on the kitchen table. It helped though, that I knew I had left them behind and were they were.

The taxi driver just asked: "Do you need it?" I said: "Yes." He then said: "When does your train leave?" I informed him of the departure time, and he said: "Okay", took the next corner and stepped on it. He never showed any sign of surprise or never even acted annoyed. Maybe this was a normal part of the job as a taxi driver. Maybe I wasn't the first customer having forgotten something important and realising it halfway to the railway station…

Having retrieved my much-needed malaria medication and fled once again down the stairs I threw myself in the taxi. At the railway station it turned out that I only had five minutes before the train would leave. The train was easy to find, so with two minutes to spare I sank down in a seat in the middle of the train. I was grateful to the taxi driver for his understanding and his driving skills. I showed my gratitude to him by giving him a generous tip. Perhaps not generous in a more general sense, but generous for being me anyway.

Apart from being angry with myself for having forgotten to pack the malaria pills, I was happy that I had planned the departure with enough margin to make the error non catastrophic. You know what they say: "What good are margins, if you don't use them" …

The rest of the trip was fortunately uneventful and I arrived at Stockholm Arlanda Airport without further hiccups. I checked in, and saw my bag disappear into the unknown insides of the facilities. I suppressed the urge to shout "See you soon!" behind the disappearing bag. I could of course have done that, followed by addressing the check-in staff with "She's more than two years old and I couldn't afford the extra ticket. Don't worry, she'll be fine. There's food and drink in there and she has Pampers' finest night-time nappy on." Somehow, I just think that this would have prevented me from catching the flight. Or any flight, for that matter. Possibly ever. Luckily, I restrained myself. There is a time and place for everything, and airports are a no-joke zone. If you want to catch a plane, that is…

So, time to spare at the airport, but I decided to locate, and go to, the gate anyway. I've seen my fair share of airports and I've compared enough prices to know that when they say "duty free" they actually mean taxes replaced in full by an increased profit margin. Alcohol and tobacco being possible exceptions to this, but I was not going home, I was going away.

Time for boarding, and I made my way to the plane. Fortunately, I had been placed by one of the emergency-exits of the Boeing 787 Dreamliner, which meant that I had a more generous space for my legs. I was given a window seat, but unfortunately there was not much view through the window in the emergency door. I had to make do with a book I brought with me, a movie from the inflight entertainment system or perhaps a little chat with the passenger in the neighbouring seat.

The plane was full. It was filled with Swedes excited to go on holiday. Since Doha is a major hub, almost everyone on the plane had connecting flights to catch for their next leg on their way to some vacation destination in Thailand or wherever. It seemed like for most of the Swedes on this flight, the vacation had started at the moment they stepped onto the plane. For many Swedes vacation equals getting drunk and staying drunk. The passengers on this flight were no exception and did nothing to prove this generalising stereotype wrong. Sitting next to the mid-section lavatories I had the privilege of watching a Swede, who clearly already had had too much to drink, trying to open the door to the lavatory carrying beer cans in both hands. What that person was intending to do when inside the lavatory with both hands occupied with the precious cargo, was a question I had no desire to delve into. I was satisfied with just deciding to not use that particular lavatory until it had been cleaned by some unfortunate flight attendant. My utmost respect and admiration go out to all of the hard-working cabin crew out there!

The person sitting next to me, in the middle seat, was a Pakistani student on his way home to surprise his family. He was studying engineering in Sweden and had not had the money to go home and see his family for the longest time, and he was very much excited to come back to Karachi to see his family again. We had a nice chat and together with a film, the six-hour flight went by and we landed at Hamad International Airport, Doha, Qatar, on time.

The waiting time at Doha Airport was 2 hours 50 minutes which gives you almost two and a half hours to walk around and discover the airport. It's a nice airport. It's new, and it has everything, but honestly, you don't need two and a half hours to check it out. But still, it was nice to be able to walk around a little and to stretch one's legs after six hours in an airplane.

We took off from Stockholm in the afternoon and it was now in the middle of the night. I didn't sleep during the last leg so I was becoming a little sleepy. This was not a bad thing, though. Maybe I would be able to get some sleep on the plane from Doha to Maputo.

I did get some sleep. Five hours of sleep (on and off), a movie and a very nice breakfast had prepared me for the arrival at Maputo International Airport.

After having showed the passport with approved visa to the immigration officer and having answered the compulsory questions of why the heck you wanted to visit their beautiful country, and giving the address of where you would be staying (I had forgotten about that, so I had to phone my friend and have him spell out his address for me), it was time for the also compulsory, and sometimes anxious wait by the conveyor belt for the checked in luggage.

When standing there I remembered a situation a number of years ago when I found myself in another baggage reclaim area waiting for my suitcase. I had arrived at Vienna International Airport, Schwechat, Austria on a LOT flight from Warsaw, Poland, together with a couple of colleagues. We were standing by the conveyor belt waiting for the belt to start moving and distributing our belongings. Nothing happened for the longest time and finally everyone from the plane had disembarked and stood there waiting. At last, the belt started moving, and everyone's eyes were fixated on the belt by the rubber curtain which separated the visible from the hidden. Suddenly something emerged on the belt from the dark and mysterious insides of the baggage handling function of the airport building. It was a pair of men's underwear. When it passed me I (who have an unfortunate habit of not keeping my mouth shut when I should) said to my colleagues, (but loud enough for others to hear,) "Someone likes to travel light!" This was found to be somewhat amusing and my colleagues chuckled and I felt rather good about myself having made this, in my opinion, clever remark.

The belt kept moving but produced nothing more. The not so surprisingly unclaimed pair of underwear disappeared through the rubber curtain at the end into the dark, and what I now understand, devious part of the building. Everyone's eyes again fixated to the point in the wall where the belt enters the room. Finally, a suitcase emerged. It was open. It was one of those hard-shell suitcases which open into two equally big halves, exposing everything packed inside. I felt bad for the owner of the suitcase. I felt even worse when I realised that I was that owner. The suitcase was actually mine.

Everyone standing beside the belt with eyes fixated at the point where the belt entered the reclaim area, had now changed their focus to see who the unfortunate person was who would claim the open suitcase. This must undoubtedly also be the owner of the previously displayed men's underwear. And, what do you know – it was none other than the guy who made the snarky remark just a moment ago!

With a face deepening in colour, I reached for the suitcase and folded it. I then quickly searched for and found the Exit-sign and started to casually (but quickly) walk towards it. I successfully defeated the urge to turn around, and like a child, in a loud voice claim "But it wasn't my underwear! It really wasn't!" I still claim that it wasn't my underwear. I really do! And I also claim that the baggage handlers at Vienna International Airport are mean people, although I should have some understanding and compassion for people who just cannot resist a temptation.

I have stored this and many other incidents in a certain part of my memory which I've labelled "Amusing experiences from a long and otherwise boring life".

Anyway, in the baggage reclaim area of Maputo International Airport my bag finally showed up. I grabbed it and prepared to, as quickly as possible, exit into the Arrival Hall, where my friend had been waiting a good while now. The plane had been somewhat delayed, and the procedures after landing had taken more time than, at least I, had expected.

No, it was not possible to just take the bag and walk out. First, I had to prove my ownership of the bag by presenting to an officer the luggage tag I got from the check-in desk in Stockholm. The officer compared the number on the tag with the number on the tag of the luggage. Then I had to allow my bag to pass through a security scanner. Then I had to show my luggage tag again to another officer who again compared the numbers on the tags. After completing this procedure, I was free to leave the baggage reclaim area, and together with a bag that undeniably belonged to me enter the Arrival Hall where my old schoolfriend was waiting.

During my wait at the different stages after landing in Maputo I had started to question if we would be able to identify each other in the Arrival Hall. We hadn't seen each other or had any visual contact for more than 45 years. Well, it turned out that two Swedes in an airport in Africa sort of stand out in the crowd. The recognition and reunion were immediate. No problem there.

It was nice of him to meet me at the airport, and we drove off towards his apartment. In the car Nils asked me about the journey and I told him about almost forgetting the malaria pills and how close this was to a disaster. Nils said something about it wouldn't have been a disaster. "You could buy the medication here" he said. To which I answered that "it requires a prescription and a visit to the doctor". He then said something like: "You don't need a prescription. You just need to know someone at the pharmacy…"

After a short sightseeing with a stop to look at the sun setting over the capital, we arrived at his apartment. He had been kind enough to offer me to stay at his place during my stay in Maputo. It turned out that his apartment was the entire eighth floor of a twelve-storey building. In the apartment was a guest bedroom with an en suite bathroom which was at my disposal during my stay with him.

As soon as I had settled in it was time for dinner. I was at that point starving, and Nils took us to a lovely restaurant nearby. So, what do two school mates talk about on their first reunion in 45 years?

Dinner topic and question no 1: "Where do you want to be buried and how would you like your funeral to be?"

This was discussed in detail (of course). It turned out that he wanted to be sent off from shore in northern Mozambique on a burning raft out on the Indian Ocean. It was my understanding that he wanted his body to be consumed by the flames on the raft. Thereby it would be cremated and he would be returned to the nature alongside the continent that he loved and considered his home.

He later adjusted his plan to make it a land-based cremation with the ashes split so that half would be spread in Mozambique and half would be spread in Sweden. I felt flattered to be there during the early stages of the planning process. Important matters like this cannot be planned too early. (Or can they?) And is there anyone better to plan your funeral with than a random schoolmate who you haven't had any contact with for the last 45 years? (Or is there?)

Anyway, for my part I said that I had to some extent discussed the different options with my children, and I had come to the conclusion that a burial at a cemetery in the town in the south of Sweden where I now live, would be the best option. This would give my children a reasonable possibility to visit my grave if that would be desired, compared to be buried in the north where none of my children (at least at the moment) live. A simple headstone would suffice, and I have money reserved in my savings account for the entire process.

But the question fails to engage me too much. I honestly

don't care. I guess that's because I assume that my funeral will be so far in the future, that I most likely will be dead by then, anyway…

After this joyful and uplifting discussion, we returned to his place for the night.

The next day after breakfast it was time for some sightseeing in Maputo. It turned out that Nils was an excellent guide. I received a lot of insightful information about Mozambique in general and Maputo in particular.

Among other interesting sights we went to Museu De História Natural de Maputo, a museum with a lot of information concerning nature and wildlife in Mozambique, and with a great number of stuffed animals. We also visited Fortaleza of Maputo, which is an old fortress. It provided us with many examples of the cruelties we humans make each other subject to. The colonial powers were in this respect more rule than exception.

It seems like we humans are constantly looking for reasons to be cruel. If someone tells us that we are on the right side, that we are "the good guys", and that we're fighting for a good cause, then we can let go of all inhibitions and just let ourselves commit any atrocity, letting our darkest and most inhuman side take control. Please, let us think for ourselves and not allow ourselves to be manipulated to a point where we unleash our inner beast.

It was a great but tiring day, and the suggestion of a short rest at the apartment before dinner was not met with any opposition.

We had dinner that evening at another pleasant nearby located restaurant.

Dinner topic and question number 2: "Illnesses and specific problems of getting older?"

Every conceivable aspect of illnesses, operations, pills, problems and pains associated with age was discussed. Special consideration was given bladder and prostate problems with in-depth penetration of the subject, and colourful descriptions of examinations and surgical procedures. A possible conclusion could be that there are not only benefits from becoming older…

However, the food was great, although the meal was finished long before the immensely interesting discussion was. It was late by the time we got back to the apartment and for some reason, I was tired.

Nils had really gone the extra mile to make my visit pleasant. Not only did he let me enjoy a sightseeing of Maputo, he had actually been able to plan a week of activities for us.

So, the next morning after breakfast we set off in his car towards Swaziland, which is a small sovereign country boarding to Mozambique to the west and is on all other sides surrounded by South Africa. After entering the country, we came across a giraffe having an early lunch from a treetop not far from the road. We also made a stop at a place where they make handmade glass objects from recycled glass bottles.

That evening, we teamed up with Francis, a friend of Nils who lives in Swaziland. He was kind enough to let us spend the night there, and the next morning we had a very nice round tour in Swaziland.

After a lovely dinner together the next day, at a golf club near Francis' home, we returned to his place to prepare for our second night under his roof. During the evening, and perhaps after a couple of drinks, I was asked about the reason for my visit to their neck of the woods. I told them of my retirement and that I wanted to explore other possibilities than just withering away in small-town Sweden. For some reason this seemed to engage the two friends and they immediately started to discuss among themselves to try to come up with something which would be more interesting for me than sitting in a sofa in Sweden waiting for time to pass. They both agreed on trying to find something interesting and exciting but still not too serious or time consuming, workwise.

– I know! Francis said suddenly. King! That's the perfect solution! That should be perfect for someone like you, and "King Karl" has a nice ring to it, don't you think!

Nils immediately agreed.

– Perfect! he said. That would be an appropriate next step in your career.

– But, a king? I said. Really!? To me that sounds a bit strange, and wouldn't that require a country of some sort to constitute like a kingdom? I'm pretty sure a king would need a kingdom. And where would that be, in that case? I think many practical questions need to be answered.

– Details, details! said Nils. You're much too concerned with unimportant details! Focus on the important things which need to be solved first, and we can sort out the boring details later.

My self-appointed royal counsellors were in total agreement, at least with each other.

– First of all, Francis continued, you'll need a suitable means of transportation. As king you would need to make state visits. We need to figure out what kind of transport you would need for that. No self-respecting king would ever go on a state visit on a bike!

The thought of King Karl arriving on a bicycle for an official state visit to a neighbouring country, raised quite a bit of laughter with the royal advisors. I found it wise to take a step back and give them space to brainstorm, and work their magic. After all, they were doing it for me, sort of…

Again, Francis came up with an idea that, at least in his mind, was the perfect solution.

– A dignified and proper transportation for a king is of course an airplane, and the perfect airplane for a small country is the de Havilland Beaver.

The royal advisors were both ecstatic over this, again, in their minds, perfect solution to a non-existing problem.

Nevertheless, I could see the benefits of the idea as such. Since this kingdom-to-be would have a very limited state budget, the Beaver could be within financial reach. It is also a plane which does not require a long runway. This could be an important feature since the country in question, once acquired, probably would be very small, and having a royal transport in the form of an airplane in need of a runway stretching across the border into a neighbouring country, could eventually give cause to a diplomatic crisis. Who would want that?

The Beaver could also be fitted with floats, and thereby suitable for landing on water, but then again, countries with a sea view are probably more expensive to acquire and therefore possibly out of reach for a king-to-be with limited financial resources.

For those not familiar with the de Havilland Beaver it can be mentioned that it is a single engine propeller aircraft with the capacity of taking up to 11 passengers, depending on model and configuration. It was manufactured by the de Havilland company in Canada between 1947 and 1967. The model was very popular as a bush-plane in remote areas due to its ability to take off and land on a short runway.

As a sidenote I must add that I very much would have liked to be a fly on the wall at the de Havilland headquarters when it was discussed what to name the aircraft. The beaver is an industrious and impressive animal with many skills, such as cutting trees and building dams, but as far as I know – its flying skills are sadly missing…

Eventually, it was getting late, and the bottle from which most of the inspiration emanated was emptied. It was time to call it a day and hit the sack, as they say.

The next morning it was time to say goodbye to Francis and go back to Mozambique and Maputo. I thought perhaps that the memory of the discussions the previous night had evaporated like the effects of the consumed bottle of inspiration, but it hadn't. The fumes were still lingering, and an ordinary goodbye turned into a royal farewell.

On our way back to Maputo we drove part of the way through South Africa. Before arriving in Maputo, we stopped at a supermarket in a commercial centre not far from the city, to buy some food and some other necessities. Well back at Nils' place we made an early night.

At the breakfast table the next morning Nils was reading the local newspaper when he suddenly showed me a short paragraph which mentioned that a large snake had been found in the dairy section of a grocery store the day before.

– That was the store which we visited, and where we made our purchases yesterday, Nils said.

Good thing that we didn't need to buy milk yesterday then…

The mission for the day was to go swimming. I was told that it's not wise to take a swim in the fresh water lakes because of the parasites living in the water. They tend to find a home and propagate in your body by entering through whatever welcoming body opening they find. They do that however small the body opening may be. I leave to your imagination to figure out the rest…

Anyway, this means that if one wants to take a swim outside, the sea is the only option. Subsequently we went to a beach about an hour drive from Maputo. Needless to say, the weather was perfect for a visit to the beach.

My plan was to continue my African adventure the next day, and since this was my last day with my friend in Maputo, a farewell dinner was in order. This dinner was to take place at a restaurant a bit outside of the city. On our way there in Nils' car, I noticed a police-check on the opposite side of the multilane road.

The idea was to have grilled prawns which was a speciality of this particular restaurant. At the table we discussed possible beverage alternatives. I then gave air to a remark concerning the police-control I had seen on our way, and which we would have to pass on our way back. I therefore suggested a bit of restraint concerning alcohol consumption, to which Nils said something like "Everything is a matter of negotiation". Anyway, we shared a bottle of Portuguese green wine, which went perfectly with the barbequed prawns.

On our way back, as we came close to the police checkpoint, I saw a policeman standing in the road. Being me, I of course gave a word of caution to my friend, to which he laughed and replied:

– If he's clever enough to become a policeman, he should be clever enough to get out of the way of a vehicle coming towards him at full speed.

He didn't slow down, and the policeman moved out of our way.

Challenging the idea of perhaps moving permanently to Africa, came the thought that maybe this was a part of the world more suitable for the likes of Nils, than for the likes of me.

Back at Nils' place, it was time for me to gather my belongings. I had to be at the airport next morning to continue my trip. Where to go next? For some reason Namibia had caught my attention. (It could just have been the Namibian beer I had tried during my stay with Nils… Sometimes the basis of our decisions is much more shallow and much less solid than we want to admit.) After finding out that I did not need a visa for entering the country I had bought a ticket for an African Airlines direct flight from Maputo to Windhoek, the capital of Namibia.

So, tomorrow I will be on a flight to continue my African adventure!

And what an adventure that would turn out to be…

Chapter 3

The airport was not too busy this morning. It was easy to move around. The airport of Maputo is well equipped to handle the number of passengers passing through, at least today. The area behind the security check line is open and spacious with access to the different gates.

I made a quick tour to the gift shop with a glance at things I possibly could have bought as gifts to my grandchildren if I were going home, which I'm not. I took a seat in the general waiting area and a young lady sitting nearby struck up a conversation with me. It turned out that she's from Ukraine and had visited Maputo where her boyfriend works, and now she was on her way back home with Turkish Airlines via Istanbul. So, what about me? Was I also going to Istanbul on the same plane?

No, not really. My intention was to go with African Airlines on AFRA314 to Windhoek, Namibia with departure time 10.15 AM. The time was now 08.05 AM. Yes, I like to be a little early.

When I went through the security check earlier, I noticed that the baggage scanner looked old and not particularly reliable. When the conveyor belt stopped and my carryon bag got stuck inside the machine, the young operator apologised to me, saying something like: "Sorry, the machine we normally use is out of order and we had to retrieve this old grumpy machine from its retirement in the storage. Unfortunately, it's not working properly and it's definitely not reliable." Whereupon a sharp voice called a name and when the young operator turned around, he received a stern look with unmistakable meaning from, what I assumed was, a supervisor. Obviously, it was not considered wise to inform the passengers, of the fact that the machine which was supposed to ensure that no dangerous objects or materials were brought into the cabin, was not working properly. I smiled and nodded and went on my merry way, pretending not to understand the implications. Since I myself felt like an old, grumpy man, not keen on being dragged out of retirement, I felt some sympathy with the poor machine.

But this was not the time to dive into the pool of self-pity. I was exploring Africa, and enjoying it. I just needed one brief moment of imagining the cold, the fog and the rain back home to make myself in the best of moods.

This incident reminded me however, of a situation which occurred when my cousin and I were taking a boat back to Spain from a visit to Morocco. At the ferry terminal outside of Tangier we were instructed to place our bags on the conveyor belt taking them through the security scanner. When the bags passed through the scanner a sharp sound of an alarm was heard and warning lights on top of the machine started rotating, calling for the attention of anyone in charge. The operating staff stood in a group together, talking, a couple of meters away from the machine. They were apparently engaged in a discussion which seemed very important to them. The reaction from the operators was subsequently in the form of disapproving faces and hand gestures ordering us to immediately take our bags and get out of there. It was obvious that they would not accept this annoying sound from the machine to disturb their interesting and possibly very important discussion. I remember thinking that their job description probably only included the part of instructing the passengers to put the baggage on the belt, but it did not give them any clue of what to do if the alarm went off… To this day I have no idea what triggered the alarm, nor have I any interest in finding out.

Had I only known then what I know now, I would have realised the actual implications of the baggage scanner not working properly and I would not have boarded the plane. Had I known when at home about what I was about to encounter on this flight I would never even have left the sad and boring, but familiar comforts of my domicile. And I would then have missed out on what would become an adventure of a lifetime. I'm such a coward! Good thing that I didn't know.

Soon it was time for boarding, and I lined up to have my boarding pass checked. The staff checking the boarding passes made sure to wish every passenger a pleasant flight. When entering the plane, I was greeted welcome by a flight attendant who had her eyes fixated at my right hand in which I held my boarding pass. I showed it to her and she confirmed what I already knew; my seat was 20F.

When I fly, I prefer to have a window seat in a row aft of the wing. I enjoy looking at the flaps being extended before take-off, and then retracted step by step once the plane is airborne. I enjoy watching the ailerons work when the plane is turning or in mid-flight as the autopilot handles the flight controls. Finally, when the plane goes in for landing the flaps extend step by step, and if the speed is not sufficiently reduced by the landing gear being extended or by other means, the speed brakes are deployed. What can I say? – I may be old, but there is in some respects also a little boy still inside me. (And anyone who knows me, could look at my impressive figure and make a comment along the lines of: "Yep. There would definitely be room for that!")

On the other hand, I seldom pay much attention to the other passengers, and this time was no exception. I was the first of the passengers to enter in the right-hand side of row number 20 (seat D – F). The next to take a seat in this part of the row was a man, possibly in his thirties who found his seat at the aisle (D). He was not more than seated, when he had to rise to his feet and step into the aisle to let the passenger of the middle seat (E) pass. This was a young girl, presumably in her teens.

As the last passengers entered the plane, I could see from my seat that it was not completely fully booked. "Why did they book three passengers in this row when there are empty seats in other rows?" I thought to myself. My legs would have enjoyed the extra space of an empty middle seat. This was of course not the fault of the passenger assigned to the middle seat, and why should I complain? It was just a little more than a two- and half-hour flight and I wouldn't let anything destroy my good moods and excitement. I was exploring Africa! This could be a game changer for me! The exhilaration connected to the prospect of changing my dull and boring life as a recently retired person, started to take over. I was exploring new, and for me unchartered territory, and I wanted to sip every last drop of this cup!

I strapped myself in, as the plane was close to fully boarded. "Boarding completed" was heard, as well as "Cabin crew: Arm doors and cross check." Soon after that, the safety demonstration began. I've seen enough of safety demonstrations in my day, but that doesn't mean that I on any flight ignore watching and listening to them. They are made for my and the other passengers' safety, and I consider it rude not to pay visible and appreciative attention to the cabin crew, as they perform this routine, perhaps for the third or fourth time today, and for the millionth time in total. Furthermore, sometimes things actually go wrong, and when they do it's often too late to start looking for "the safety card situated in the seat pocket in front of you". (It's almost impossible for me to think of the phrase "situated in the seat pocket in front of you" without the voice in my head sounding like a flight attendant…)

So, I took out the safety card "situated in the seat pocket in front of me" (oh, stop it, already!) and noted among other things that this was a Boeing 737-700. That means that it is a fairly recent model, also known as a New Generation, or 737 NG.

The 737 NG-series is rather new, but still designed before the Boeing management decided that it was more important to build a plane that could sell, rather than to make it safe to fly.

There had been two deadly crashes involving brand new Boeing 737 MAXs. The first one being a Lion Air crash in Indonesia in October 2018, and the second one being an

Ethiopian Airlines crash outside Addis Ababa, Ethiopia in March 2019, in total killing 346 passengers and crew.

When the news about the crashes were spread around the world, we were told that the 737 MAX was the fastest-selling plane in the history of Boeing, with over 5 000 orders in the book. To me that was an indication of how the management of Boeing saw the matter.

Soon after the first crash there were rumours and speculations concerning the involvement, or possible malfunction, of a system called MCAS. Information about this system was hard to find since neither airlines nor pilots were informed of its existence, and in consequence, they were in the dark on what to do if it for any reason malfunctioned, or was erroneously activated. The questions about the system were therefore directed at Boeing.

I could almost picture a press conference where reporters were asking representatives of Boeing what MCAS was and what its function was. Then there could have been a long and detailed explanation involving bigger, more fuel efficient and more powerful engines, changed position of the engines, and the plane behaving differently in certain situations compared to previous versions of the 737, which in turn could lead to a risk of entering a stall situation, etc., etc., and hence the need for a software to prevent this from happening. "So, it's a stall prevention system, is it?" "Yes, you could say that." "So basically, it's a safety system?" The Boeing representatives could have liked this way of describing it; 'a safety system for stall prevention' not bad, not bad at all!

If a plane's pitch is too high relative to its speed, the wings can lose sufficient lift, and the plane risk entering an aerodynamic stall, and thereby "drop to the ground like a stone". The function of the system was to lower the nose of the plane if it sensed that the plane was nearing such a situation. The information fed to the system was, among other sources, a vane on the side of the plane called an angle of attack sensor, or AOA-sensor for short. The 737 has two AOA-sensors, one on each side of the fuselage.

As it turned out, MCAS had one major shortcoming and one unfortunate ability. The shortcoming being that the system relied on information from just one AOA-sensor. There are, as mentioned, two sensors, but only one at a time fed information to the MCAS system. The unfortunate ability of the system was that of its power. If the system for any reason was triggered to push the nose of the plane down, it was able to do so regardless of the actions of the pilots. The system was relentless, and the activity of the system had to be turned off if erroneously triggered, in order to prevent it from sending the plane to a complete nosedive, which in turn would result in what was in one document described as a "possible impact with terrain", aka a crash.

A while later, but still in the middle of all investigation and all of the discussions concerning the possible causes of the crashes, some reporter somewhere came to the conclusion that if MCAS is a stall prevention system needed on the MAX model, this would mean that the design of the plane must be inherently unstable. When Boeing got wind of this interpretation, they blew a company gasket: "The 737 MAX is not inherently unstable!! MCAS is designed to do exactly what the acronym stands for: Manoeuvring Characteristics Augmentation System. This means that the system will ensure that despite the changes to the design of the 737, the manoeuvring characteristics would be the same as for previous version of the 737, so that no additional pilot training would be necessary."

Pilot training is time consuming and therefore costly for the airlines, i.e., Boeing's customers. If the training needed would require simulator training, that would mean even more costs in upgrading existing simulators or even building new ones. But on the other hand, if additional training were not to be needed for the 737-pilots in order to be able to fly the MAX, it would subsequently not increase the total cost of acquiring the airplane, and would thereby be a major sales argument.

Congratulations Boeing! Apparently the poorly designed and poorly thought-through MCAS is not a safety system gone wrong. It's a sales argument gone wrong! In what way is that expected to inspire confidence in the plane manufacturer, I wonder?

To make matters worse, the Boeing CEO at the time, Muilenburg, looked straight into the camera and addressed the public with the words; "We've always been relentlessly focused on safety, and always will be. It's at the very core of who we are at Boeing." I remember thinking that I hope with all my heart that this is a lie. If this statement is anywhere near the truth, it would mean that although every employee at Boeing would be "relentlessly focused on safety", yet no one at the company, no one, stopped for a moment to think; "what if". What if a cable comes loose? What if there is a short circuit? What if the AOA-sensors' movements are blocked by sand from a sandstorm, by ice in the arctic or by a sloppy paintjob, so that they can't move and send correct information? What if there's a bird strike?

What if the AOA-sensors themselves malfunction and start to send incorrect readings to the computer? What then? Is there a need for a backup system? Maybe a warning to the pilots? Why not use information from more than just one AOA-sensor? Why not use information from both AOA-sensors if they are in agreement. If they are not in agreement, the MCAS-system could disconnect with a warning to the pilots. This would of course mean that the pilots had to be informed about the existence of the system… Ooppss…

Is it really in alignment with "being relentlessly focused on safety" to withhold, from the airlines and the pilots, essential safety information about the design of the plane, and to do so possibly to support sales, based on the promise that the MAX behaves exactly like the previous version of the 737? If this is the best that Boeing employees can do when they are "relentlessly focused on safety" being as it is "at the very core of who we are at Boeing", then there is nothing that can save this company, because then each and every one of the employees is helplessly incompetent.

I'm not an engineer. I'm not a flight mechanic, and I'm not a pilot. I'm just a member of the flying public. But even I, having no experience or knowledge in the field of aviation whatsoever, even I know that every crucial flight control system has backup systems. Not just one backup system, often at least two. So, if I, an accountant, and a complete nincompoop when it comes to airplanes, can understand that having a system installed that has the potential to bring the plane to a nosedive and thereby cause the death of everyone on board, and this system relies solely on one source of information, namely one of the plane's two angle of attack sensors, and no one, except for the people behind their desks at Boeing, know about the existence of this system – basically that is not a good idea. Is this the best that skilled engineers and devoted professionals can come up with when being "relentlessly focused on safety"? I refuse to believe that.

If, on the other hand, co-workers at Boeing are under pressure from the management, which in turn is receptive only to one type of information, namely information provided by the sales department, then in that case, I think it could be possible to save the company. It will take years, cost a huge amount of money and it will take a most dedicated and specific effort from the management. The problem with that, as I see it, is that the management in this case, is the cause and the root of the problem. So, my conclusion is that Boeing either needs a new management mind-set, or an entirely new management. The only way to save the company, again, as I see it, is to purposely, meticulously and "relentlessly" revive a safety culture which no doubt once was at "the core" of the company and its co-workers. But, in order to manage to do that, it also takes an organisation designed to effectively identify and deal with potential non-adherence to the core values of quality, safety and engineering excellence. This part of the organisation must have direct and unfiltered access to the top management in order to be effective. This in turn means that the managers themselves must regard these values as non-negotiable core values, and act upon them as such. The board of directors are, after all, ultimately responsible for, among other things, the culture in, and the performance of, the company. And that's where my doubts set in. How much dedication concerning this can you expect from a management which has so blatantly neglected one of its basic obligations?

It should not be necessary to point out that there is a difference between running a company which manufactures office supplies, on one hand, and running an American world-leading airplane manufacturer, on the other. One can be treated solely as a money-making machine without major life-threatening ramifications, while the other requires much more sincere considerations.

It's one of the more basic truths, that in order to actually solve a problem, it's not enough to deny its existence and say: "Problem? What problem? We don't have a problem!" On the contrary, it's necessary to accept the existence of the problem, to fully acknowledge it, and to assess it, and then to evaluate its impact, in order to be able to find the appropriate means to resolve it.

Yes, I know that the management of Boeing has been forced to take some steps and make some changes after this debacle. To an outsider, it seems though, as if the management has delt with the need for renewal of the company in the same way they delt with the need for a replacement of the then 40-year-old 737; "We don't actually need it." It appears like the easiest and cheapest solution is chosen, without proper analysis and/or understanding of the problem. The changes made seem to only serve the purpose of the management being able to say: "Look, we've taken measures. Look, we've actually done something!"

It's been said before, but it's worth repeating; MCAS was not the problem, it was merely the symptom of an underlying problem. That problem will continue to affect the company and its products until it is resolved.

I don't want to think of Boeing in twenty- or thirty-years' time being reduced to making spare parts for the Russian and/or Chinese aviation industry. Not that I would be around, but still…

Oh dear, I sort of made myself a bit worked up there… My eyes fell again on the safety card and its comforting statement that this was a Boeing 737-700, designed and manufactured before the current management of Boeing succeeded to steer this once so respected company and its products in a dire direction.

The plane taxied and lined up at the end of the runway. After a short wait apparently take-off clearance was given by the tower, the engines spooled up, the brakes were released, and we speeded down the runway. I had of course prepared myself for this, my favourite moment, and I had adjusted myself in my seat. I could therefore feel the backrest press against my back as we accelerated, and shortly after, I could feel the seat cushion press against my legs at lift-off. This was a smooth take-off and we were now on our way. Soon we would land in Windhoek, Namibia. I leaned back, and allowed myself to enjoy the ride.

About twenty minutes into the flight, I saw some activity in the front of the galley. It seemed like the cabin crew was preparing for the distribution of coffee, tea and other refreshing drinks. I wouldn't say no to a cup of coffee, even though I knew from experience that this would mean a visit to the lavatory after a short while. The Boeing 737-700 in this configuration had two lavatories, one in the front of the cabin, next to the galley and one in the back. Apart from the apparent preparing for beverage distribution, I noticed that there seemed to be a queue to the lavatory, as I could see three of the passengers seemingly waiting outside the lavatory close to the galley.

Suddenly there was a bit of commotion, followed by what appeared to be angry and agitated but slightly muffled arguing in the front. A few moments later and the situation was made clear to me and to the rest of the passengers – the plane had been hijacked.

This was made clear in no uncertain terms by a person who stood in front of the cabin and shouted something in a language I couldn't identify and even less understand. The message was clear though, and emphasised by the waving of something in his hand that looked like a piece of plastic, but apparently was meant to scare us into submission. It could possibly be some homemade device for shooting bullets. I don't know. I'm not an expert in firearms nor in the making of them. Was it dangerous? Probably. I for one had no interest in checking out its capabilities.

So, we were actually hijacked, and we were most probably going to die. I felt an ice-cold hand reach into my chest and grab my heart and squeeze it. I had trouble breathing and my mind was racing. Nothing of value presented itself from my intense brain activity, though. The message my brain at this stage succeeded to convey was: "We're going to die! We're going to die! We're going to die! We're going to die!" Big help that was…

I've sometime thought that some of us carry sort of an anxiety gauge inside. In my case I picture it being round with a white bottom, a needle to tell the level of anxiety and at the end of the scale a pin to stop the needle's progress. The scale is divided into three parts; a green, a yellow and a red part. When the needle dwells in the green area, everything is fine. There is not a worry in the world, the sun is shining, and there is no need to be anxious. When something is potentially dangerous, the needle enters the yellow part. There, the level of attention is heightened and one becomes more focused and concentrated, prepared to react on whatever may happen. When the needle moves into the red zone, that's where the real stress begins; the sweating starts, the heart starts racing, the mind spins or locks and the tunnel vision sets in. This state of irrational defence grows worse and worse the deeper into the red area the needle progresses. At the far end of the red zone there is just utter and uncontrollable panic.

But, just before the needle comes to rest against the pin at the end of the scale, there is a little gap between the red area and the stopping pin. That's where the white bottom colour of the gauge is seen. This is also where everything becomes different. The sweating stops, the stomach unties its knot, the mind becomes extremely focused and crystal clear, and all types of emotions disappear. This is when instinct replaces emotion as part of, or basis for, the decision making. This is when one becomes lethal, emotionless and instinct-driven.

After a while my breathing slowly became more normal, as did my heartrate, and my brain started to question its previous conclusion. Maybe we were not going to die. Maybe these were kind and friendly hijackers. Maybe they were just some friends who wanted to go somewhere but couldn't afford the air fare, so they bought tickets for a cheaper flight with the plan to hijack the plane and force the pilot to fly to the destination of their choice, at which point they, after landing, would thank us for the ride, and apologise for the inconvenience, and wish us the best, and then just trod off. This was definitely a possibility.

I held on to that thought until one of the two hijackers walked along the aisle, checking up on us, apparently to make sure that no one was up to anything. I looked at him, and this man's face was not the face of a man who had apologised for anything during the last two decades. It was the face of a man who was used to demand apologies of others, and not in a nice way.

They were a bit different the two hijackers. The one walking up and down the aisle looked like the one in charge of the two. He looked like a professional. He seemed to be in his mid-thirties, well built, fit, and well trained. His total appearance made it absolutely clear that he would not accept any arguing from anyone. The other hijacker who remained in front of the cabin by the galley was much younger and looked much less self-assured than the other. He appeared to be around twenty and looked more like a lost boy who, for whatever reason, had started to hang out with the wrong people. I suspected that the boy's mother would have a thing or two to say about the predicament her son had put himself into. From time to time, it appeared like the only thing he wanted was to go home to see his mother and then to just stay there. Unfortunately, he now found himself in a situation he couldn't get out of at thirty thousand feet and not knowing exactly what to do. Fortunately (or whatever the correct word might be), his older accomplice knew exactly what to do, for both of them. I still wondered what the young man's mother would have to say about his present activity.

But wait, didn't I see three men outside the lavatory by the galley in front of the cabin? Who was the third person? Was that a more or less innocent passenger waiting in line to the lavatory with an overfilled bladder, or was that a third hijacker? If he was one of the hijackers, where was he now? And where was the cabin crew?

At this point my mind had returned to its original thought; that we were going to die, and it started to make preparations for this scenario. Of course, there were other possibilities. Any number of developments and different outcomes could be plausible, but to me in that situation the thought of imminent death was the least stressful. Starting to hope and then lose hope, and then to start hoping again and in all that, continuously calculate probabilities… Nope. Settling with the thought that we were all going to die gave me some sort of peace of mind. It made my mind clearer, oddly enough, and it made it possible for me to assess the situation and to more fully take in what was happening around me without constantly calculating the possibilities of different outcomes.

Don't get me wrong. I'm just as afraid of dying as anyone else. I have the same instinct of self-preservation as the next man. It's just that the concept of death fills me with more curiosity than fright. For anyone who is interested in travel, visiting places one has never visited before, and experiencing things for the first time, death is the ultimate journey. No one knows what happens after we die. No one. There are a large number of people who claim that they do know, but I don't believe them. This is partly because these people seem to think it most important to contradict others who have different beliefs. I bought a book on the subject of death a couple of years ago, a book which I actually have read. It contained page after page describing different beliefs and belief systems concerning death and what happens after we die. On every other page though, the author stated what we all know, and have known from the beginning; and that is that we don't know what happens when we die. To be able to write a whole book stating what everyone knows before reading it, is quite an achievement. As for me – I'm not buying that book again…

But I had peace with God, so that was a check. Yes, I believe in God, so sue me! Next question was my loved ones. Had I told my children that I love them? Possibly… But hey, if I hadn't, they're not stupid, they must have figured that out by themselves by now, right? Could I send them a message from my mobile? Was that even technically possible? What would I write? "Hi, I'm on a plane in Africa. It's been hijacked and we're probably all going to die. Have a nice and long life and please say hi to your mom from me." "PS. If it's too complicated or expensive to transport my remains to Sweden, just sod it. I don't care." Would that be a message to brighten their day and make life easier for them? This is a tricky one, because they are possibly more upset about my passing, than I am.

The question whether I should try to send a text message to my children or not demanded serious consideration. I weighed pros and cons. The pros of course having to do with the general courtesy of passing on important information. We all have a basic interest in being informed of things that may, or may not, affect us in the present, or in the future. The cons were more a consideration of the children's present wellbeing. If it were at all possible to send them a message similar to the one mentioned above, they would probably be upset, but they wouldn't be able to do anything about it. It would just upset them and then they would have to wait for confirmation in one form or the other regarding the outcome. That must feel like torture for them. Then there was also the possibility of a totally positive outcome. In that case it would be even worse to have sent a message that would have upset them for no other reason than a "general courtesy of passing on important information."

I had my mobile set to flight-mode in the pocket of my cargo-trousers but I decided not to try using it. If the outcome of the situation would be as I expected it to be, they would be upset when they were informed, but better later than sooner. Right or wrong, that was my assessment and decision anyway, and if by any chance we would experience a more positive outcome; at least they weren't misinformed by me. Regardless of how this situation would end, I believe my children will be thankful that I'm withholding the information. I think that they will be grateful that they could live one more day in blissful ignorance of my predicament. I can't deny that I felt rather pleased with myself and my thoughtful decision.

My reaction to the present situation reminds me of something that happened just the other day. I think I mentioned that one of the days I spent in Mozambique, Nils and I went to a beach.

When we arrived at the beach, we saw that we were alone at this particular part of the beach. One could see in the far distance what looked like a family with two minor children. That was all. We changed into swimming trunks and I saw my friend who was faster than I (he's not an accountant) lay down on the sand close to the water letting the waves wash against him. After being thoroughly rinsed by the sea he then moved to lay down in the sand, four or five meters further up on the bank to dry up.

After having changed into swimming trunks, as well as having meticulously folded my clothes and placed them out of reach for unwanted sand (I'm an accountant), I thought I'd go and have a proper bath. I would have liked to say "go for a swim" but since I can barely stay afloat for a short period of time, much less swim, I cannot pretend that actual swimming was my aim.

It was not particularly windy that day and the waves were not particularly high, maybe around half a meter or so. Perfect to walk out into the water a bit and then let the waves wash the parts of the body not already submerged. Maybe even lay down and try to float a bit in the water and if the waves would feel too aggressive, just let the feet find grip on the sand at the bottom and walk closer to shore.

That was my plan, but this was not how events would play out. I approached the edge were the sand met the sea and when I came close, the edge just gave way. My foot and my leg disappeared down into the water and the rest of my body had no choice but to follow. I couldn't even feel the bottom, it was deeper than I was tall. So, now was the time to try to remember how to float and possibly also how to swim. This was of course just beside the sandy beach. How bad could it be?

A wave that had rolled onto the beach moved out again and took me with it. Now the situation became a little bit more exciting than a couple of seconds ago. I tried my best to swim, and luckily another wave took me back to the edge of the beach again, so now everything was great! I could touch the sand with my hand and so it would be a piece of cake to get back on the beach.

In some parts of the west coast of Sweden and also in Denmark, the grains of sand are so fine that with a little bit of moist the sand becomes hard as concrete. You can drive your car on it and people frequently park their cars on the beach by the water when they go swimming.

This was not the case with this sand. Here the grains were big, between one and two millimetre in size, and it was impossible to get a grip. The wave withdrew and took me with it. Another wave took me back towards the beach and I tried again to grip the sand. I buried my hands in the sand as deep as I could, but to no avail. When the wave retracted out to sea, so did I. A third time same situation, same method, same result. By this time, I had swallowed some water and I realised that I literally was in over my head and the thought came to me; "Is this it?" "Is this how my life is going to end?" "Am I about to drown in the Indian Ocean outside the coast of Mozambique?" "OK, so if this is it, then at least it's better than dying from a heart attack at home." "Indian Ocean?" "OK." "But if I drown, my friend will be really upset when he discovers my dead body floating in the water."

I eventually managed to get enough grip from the sand to withstand the power of the water trying to pull me back out again, and I could crawl back up on the sandy beach, and all was fine.

I was probably never in any real danger, and it turned out fine in the end, but it definitely scared me for a moment, nevertheless. What struck even me as odd, when I later thought about the incident, was the fact that even though my brain went in the "I could die" -mode and all of the thoughts that followed, never once did I consider asking my friend for help. He was a few meters away and I was maybe a meter out in the water at most. It would have meant nothing for him to help me out. He could have just come down and stretched out a hand and helped me in and up onto the shore. No time or sweat involved whatsoever. And yet, that thought never even entered my mind. Instead, my thought was "I'm possibly going to drown. If I do, he will be upset when he discovers it."

It could possibly be that my subconscious realised that I wasn't in any life-threatening danger at all. That could well be, but I still find my reaction a bit strange. That was my reaction at that time, and in that situation. There is no telling how I would react if another life-threatening situation would occur. Or maybe, that's what I'm about to find out.

When the hijacker who was obviously in charge, marched patrolling up and down the aisle, I tried, as inconspicuously as I could, to get a better look at the thing he carried in his hand. It was presumably regarded as a weapon by the hijacker or at least something that we, the passengers, would, or rather should, perceive as a weapon. But what was it? It looked like a piece of plastic. The only explanation I could come up with was that it could be a sort of firearm made in some composite material and designed for firing one single bullet. I believe I could see like a barrel opening in front of the thing, even though the barrel itself must be very short. This would make it very difficult to aim and hit anything farther away than, let's say, four or five meters. If my assumptions were correct, this could not, by any stretch, be regarded as a precision weapon, but it was still scary enough if one stood face to face with it.

My mind had started to organise my thoughts. Thought number one was established:

1. We are going to die.

Thought number two was forming in my mind, and came out as:

2. Is there anything I can do for anyone else to ease their pain or to comfort them in their last moments? Just anything.

The situation gave little room for me to do anything for anyone. The thought of my loved ones was ready and checked. I was not going to try to send them a message and with that I would keep them from worrying. Anyone else? There was only one person I would be able to do anything for and that was the person sitting next to me, in the middle seat. This was, as I previously mentioned, a young girl. I could tell that she was distraught. I could see in the corner of my eye that she was breathing heavily as well as constantly and nervously changing her position in the seat. When the hijacker was passing our row, checking on us, she curled up and I had the impression that she wanted to make herself invisible.

I nudged her with my elbow, but I had to do it three times, to get her attention. She was apparently so scared that she was unable to process information from outside. When I finally had her attention, I used my own, at that point made up, sign language, to ask her if she wanted to switch seat with me. The only thing I could think of to do for her was to let her sit one more seat farther away from the patrolling hijacker. This would not change her life in any way, but perhaps it could make her feel up to one percent better. (I'm an accountant and sometimes we like to calculate in percentages.) This was my hope and wish for her and all that I could do. She looked grateful enough, and nodded in acceptance of the offer, but looked as though she wondered how this change would be performed. So did I.

Normally if one wants to change seat with someone on a plane, it's rather simple. Every party concerned steps out of the row into the aisle, switches position until everyone is satisfied, and then returns to the row in a new and hopefully better arrangement. This is, for obvious reasons, not possible in a hijacking/hostage situation.

I looked at the distance between my knees and the backrest in front; five centimetres. Seven at the most. Still too narrow.

Whatever one wanted to do, it had to be done when the hijackers were otherwise occupied, or at least not looking in our direction. After a while, something in the galley caught their attention and kept them occupied, so I decided that it was now or never. I unbuckled my seatbelt and pointed at hers to make her understand that she had to unbuckle herself as well. I raised the armrest between us with my elbow and slid ever so slowly onto the space between our seats. I turned my legs towards her as she moved her legs away from mine. This created enough space between my knees and the seats in the row in front, for her to move herself on top of my legs. She understood the importance of keeping her head low so she did a good job in not drawing attention to herself. We were now in a critical stage, and time was of the essence. At any moment whatever had kept the hijackers occupied in the galley, could cease to keep them occupied, and they would probably immediately spot our unauthorised activity. I threw caution to the wind and grabbed her with both hands by her waist and helped her to land in the window seat while I simultaneously slid into the middle seat. I noticed her fastening her seatbelt. There was apparently a bit of seatbelt adjustment for her to do, for some reason… Anyway, mission accomplished! I slowly, again with my elbow, lowered the armrest between our seats. I glanced at her. She was looking out the window. I had the impression that her body was a little less tense than before.

Of course, the change of seats had no impact whatsoever on her overall situation, but it could possibly make her a tiny bit less stressed now that she was a little bit farther away from the threats. I thought to myself that if we were to end up in a situation where the hijackers would start picking out and executing random passengers in order to put pressure on possible negotiators, she would be slightly better off sitting in a window seat. At least that was a thought, that made me feel better.

Luckily, we had been able to perform the manoeuvre without catching the attention of anyone. Our row was in the rear of the plane, but still not the last row. There is always a risk in a situation like this, that someone who wants to score points with the people currently in power, would draw their attention to any behaviour deemed to be rebellious.

N.B. This manoeuvre is to be performed in very specific airplane hijacking situations only! Also please note, that there are height, weight and age restrictions to be considered! This can be exemplified and made clear just by exercising the thought of you switching seat on an airplane with your aunt Heather, being as she is both old as well as oversized in all directions…

The next question was if I could possibly do something for my new neighbour to the left, the man in the aisle seat. I glanced at him. He didn't strike me as someone who was pleading for help or assistance of any kind. He appeared to be in his thirties, well built, fit and had the looks of someone working with a police force or in the army. His appearance gave the impression that he both could, and wanted, to take care of himself.

His behaviour was interesting though, and actually in line with my previous assumption concerning his profession and/or abilities. When the hijackers were looking in our direction, he slumped in his seat, looked unengaged and generally sort of scared and useless. (It just has to be said that his acting was poor. He was clearly not an actor, and any award for his performance was not to be expected. Fortunately, the hijackers were not theatre critics in any capacity and apparently failed to notice.) On the other hand, when the hijackers were not looking, he was sitting up and looking around as if he was counting rows, memorising every detail of our environment, and assessing those of the passengers he was able to see from his position, as to determine who could be of help, who could be a threat, and who would just be in the way.

At this point my brain launched another thought to go with the first two, since (1) we were most probably going to die and (2) there was apparently nothing I could do for anyone else:
3. Is there anything I can do to make it as hard as possible for the hijackers to do us harm?

This was not a thought that stood unchallenged. I would think that some people that I've come across during my life would consider me as someone who is responsible, and willing to take on responsibility. This is actually not quite true. It is true that I have taken on responsibility when I've been forced to do so, but generally I've been avoiding responsibility all my life.

Why would I engage myself in our current situation? It had got nothing to do with me, apart from the fact that I would probably die together with everyone else on the plane. But I had neither caused the problem, nor was it specifically directed at me. Why bother? Worst case scenario; if I did something stupid, I could in fact make our imminent death even more imminent. Or, if I made the slightest mistake, I could cause injury to, or death of, another innocent passenger. Would I really be willing to take that responsibility? There were a lot of passengers on this flight. Why not just sit back and see what happens, like all of the others? Taking responsibility is taking a risk, and I'm not a risk taker. I like to play it safe. I don't like to be exposed, neither to risk nor otherwise.

Shakespeare's immortal words came to mind: "Whether 'tis nobler in the mind to suffer the slings and arrows of outrageous fortune, or to take arms against a sea of troubles…"

No, I haven't read Shakespeare. It's just one of those popular and well-known quotes one can casually use, to make oneself perceived as being educated and sophisticated. The wording of the quote is in this situation reasonably fitting, though.

So basically, I guess it boils down to the questions: Who do I want to be, and who do I dare to be? Am I willing to take the risk of assuming any kind of responsibility for the situation I currently find myself in? How much of a coward am I?

My decision in the matter came gradually. I just did not want to sit idly by and wait and see what may or may not come. I wanted to act on thought no. 3; to do anything at all that would make it as hard as possible for the hijackers to do us harm.

Of course, noticing my next-seat neighbour apparently planning something, unclear what, did help in making my decision. I wasn't alone. If he was up to something, I would want to be a part of it. I think… Perhaps…

Anyway, I leaned towards him and whispered:

– If you are going to do something, I can follow behind you.

He in turn leaned towards me and whispered back:

– Je ne parle pas Anglais !

Oh, goodie! French! And he doesn't speak English! Interesting snag, but then again, possible to overcome. I only needed to retrieve my knowledge in French from school not more than 50 years ago! Maybe I should have made another decision… Suddenly, sitting back and waiting for things to develop, seemed like a tempting alternative.

Nevertheless, I started to compose a sentence that would be reasonably correct and hopefully possible for him to understand. I started off with "Si tu vas faire…" Nope, too informal. I was not on first name basis with this man. Although this was a life-threatening situation, there was no reason to be impolite. Or, grammatically incorrect, for that matter. I struggled with my somewhat hazy memory of French grammar and came up with:

– Si vous allez faire quelque chose, je peux vous suivre.

I felt rather pleased with myself for my achievement in putting together such an, in my mind, flawless sentence, and I eagerly awaited his reaction. There was none. Not a glance, not a nod, not a pat on the leg. Nothing. At first, I was both disappointed and annoyed. Not only did I get zero recognition for my efforts in the French language, but apparently, he did not even appreciate my offer to assist him.

After a while I started to consider his possible point of view. I wouldn't hold it against him if his thoughts were more in line with: "Wow, this must be my lucky day! The fat old man sitting beside me says that if I'm going to do something he can follow. Well, then I'd better not move too fast, so that he will be able to keep up…"

I noticed how he had folded the seatbelt and put the straps on top of each other in his lap, so that it would look like it was locked although it wasn't, just as I myself had done. I think that he also had raised his left armrest, the one towards the aisle. My left armrest, the one between his and my seat, was also raised at this point. He maybe didn't want my "'elp", but I wanted to be prepared anyway for all eventualities.

The hijacker commenced another inspection-walk along the aisle. He walked slowly, giving every row a thorough stare, left and right. When he came to row 20, our row, he stopped a little longer, glaring at the passengers in seats E and F. His otherwise cold and emotionless face now showed a glimpse of confusion. There was definitely something different about that row, but he was, fortunately for us, unable to figure out what it was. I looked up at him and tried to look innocent and stupid. This was no stretch for me, although the innocent part required some acting. The Frenchman (or whatever nationality he was) slumped in his seat as usual. The bad acting from his (and my) part would have been spotted by someone with ability to detect inadequate acting skills, and the unlocked seatbelts would have been spotted by the trained eye of a flight attendant. Fortunately, the hijacker lacked the skill and training in both for him so important areas, and he was subsequently unable to detect what he would soon be aware of being a direct threat to him and the entire operation.

Finally, he decided that he had glared enough and moved slowly towards row 21, the row behind us. Just as he had passed our row and positioned himself to inspect the next row, the Frenchman (or whatever nationality he was), jumped out of his seat, tripped the hijacker, and attacked him from behind. I froze. I could see the young hijacker in the front of the cabin doing the same. His facial expression was that of bewilderment, distrust and confusion. Apparently, he had not anticipated this turn of events. He could hardly believe it and he didn't know what to do. The two fighting men were now on the aisle floor, the Frenchman (or whatever nationality he was), on top, and both fighting desperately. I saw the young hijacker in front slowly raising his weapon towards the two fighting men, with the back of the attacker totally exposed.

If the hijacker were to fire his weapon and hit my seat-companion's back, it would all be over. But what could

I do? I knew I had to unfreeze, but what could I actually do? I had promised the Frenchman (or whatever nationality he was) to follow, but what good would that do? The last time I was in a fight was in fourth grade, and that was a very, very, very long time ago. I was ten at the time and I can't even remember why I fought the other boy. I can't remember who won, but I have a vague recollection of a teacher breaking us up. I had nothing to offer in this fight, but still, I couldn't just sit there and wait for my fellow passenger to get a bullet in his back, and the hijackers to resume their malicious activity.

I suddenly realised that I actually had one thing to offer. I jumped out of my seat, out into the aisle and stood or kneeled (can't remember which) behind the two fighting men to try to shield the back of the Frenchman (or whatever nationality he was) from a possible bullet, with my body. I prepared myself for the feeling of having my back penetrated by a bullet, although I realised that if the hijacker shot his only bullet into me, he would actually have gained nothing. The fight would still go on, and he himself would have lost his (presumably) only bullet.

That's when I saw it. The fighting hijacker on the floor had dropped his weapon when he fell. It lay on the aisle floor half a meter in front of him, but out of his reach. He was desperately trying to reach it, as he equally desperately tried to free himself from the grips of his attacker.

I made my decision in a fraction of a second. I left my shielding position and leaped over the fighting men, aiming for the weapon. Don't ask me how I did that. My body and I, we don't run, we don't jump and my leap-years, if ever I had any, are long time over. I just guess that's what dire straits and adrenaline does for you… (And with dire straits I mean the situation, not Dire Straits the band.) I landed on the other side of the two fighters, my left hand found the weapon, I swung around on one knee, and grabbed the weapon with both hands. I could see the face of the young hijacker in the front. He had taken a few steps towards us but his face was now not only showing bewilderment and confusion but also fear. I saw him raising his weapon in our direction. I prayed, I aimed, and my index finger found a protruding lever or knob on the side of the weapon. I pressed it, hoping that it was the trigger. It was. The gun went off, and I could see the face of the young hijacker change to express sheer surprise as he fell forward and landed face down on the aisle floor. I prayed I hadn't killed him. I definitely did not want to kill him, but I felt that there was nothing else I could do in that situation, but to fire the weapon at him.

The two men in front of me were still fighting, but it appeared that the Frenchman (or whatever nationality he was) was working his way towards subduing the hijacker.

I rose to my feet and made my way past the two men on the floor. I continued towards the front of the aisle and passed the young hijacker lying face down on the aisle floor. He was not moving, and blood was starting to show on the floor beneath his body. I know I should have stopped and checked to see if he was still alive, but I just could not make myself do that. I don't know how to check for vital signs, although I realise that it shouldn't be too complicated, but at the same time I also realised that I had other important things to attend to; like finding the cabin crew. Dead or alive, the hijacker was lying still, and even if he was dying,

I wouldn't know what to do to save him. Maybe one of the cabin crew would know more than I did. That was my hope at the time, anyway.

I picked up the weapon which the hijacker had dropped when he fell, put it in the side pocket of my cargo trousers, and continued to the galley where I located the cabin crew. The purser and the two flight attendants were sitting on the floor with their hands behind their backs. The purser was sitting in the front, looking up at me. I bowed down and bent his upper body forward so that I could have a look at his arms and hands. Cable ties. I did the same check with the flight attendants. All were handcuffed with cable ties. Cable ties! Just my luck! No, this was not the time for self-pity. I was not the one sitting on the galley floor with my hands tied behind my back. Surely there must be something on the plane I could use to cut them open. I asked the purser.

– No, we don't carry anything sharp on the plane. For security reasons, he said.

– But surely a pair of scissors?

– No knives, no scissors, nothing sharp.

This was becoming ridiculous. One hijacker subdued. I turned and looked at the back of the aisle to confirm my assumption. Yes, by the look of it, finally subdued, and one hijacker deadly wounded, but hopefully still alive. And yet, all cabin crew with their hands tied with cable ties behind their backs and nothing to free them with.

– The only tool we have on this flight is a tiny screwdriver I keep in the inner pocket of my jacket, the purser said. It's just something I carry in case I can do some simple repair on the electric or electronic equipment we have in the galley. He looked sad and apologetic.

I nodded. I just didn't know what to do. I was out of ideas. I reached to the inner pocket of his jacket, just the same, and pulled out a miniscule screwdriver. I looked at it. This screwdriver was the perfect tool if your predicament could be solved by unscrewing the screws on the remote control of your television set. Unfortunately, this predicament was of a different kind, and much more severe.

But wait, had I not been able to loosen a cable tie just like these, a number of years ago, by using a similar tool? I decided to give it a try. I knelt by the purser, pushing his back forward to give me room, and forced the tiny screwdriver into the back of the lock of the cable tie. With the screwdriver in position, I managed to lift the little tongue of the locking mechanism, thereby opening the tie and thus freeing the captive.

Perfect! We now had one free purser and one perfectly operational cable tie to be used at our discretion. I asked the purser to bring the cable tie to the Frenchman (or whatever nationality he was) who by now was occupied holding the hijacker in, what appeared to me, being some sort of a policeman's grip.

– Try to tie it around his ankles, unless the passenger tells you otherwise. Just make sure it's really tight. I said.

I don't know why I gave orders like that, but I guess someone had to. The purser looked at me and nodded. He looked somewhat grateful. Apparently, he didn't mind taking orders, at least as long as it came from someone he deemed trustworthy.

– On your way back here, please check on the other guy on the floor, I said. And if you can, see if he is alive and if he is, see if you can do anything to keep him alive. Try to stop his bleeding or something. I'll untie the flight attendants.

I attended to the attendants, repeating the method I had used with the purser's cable tie. They looked grateful as they were freed, but scared and bewildered and lost. That was my feelings exactly, but nothing I intended to show those who thought they could rely on me.

I took the two cable ties which constituted the loot from the rescue operation, and set off to the situation at the rear of the plane. By now a number of passengers had joined the Frenchman (or whatever nationality he was), and a couple of them actually helped in keeping the hijacker restrained. This allowed the Frenchman (or whatever nationality he was) to make use of one of the cable ties I presented him with. The other cable tie I reserved for the other hijacker if he would regain consciousness and become violent. Somehow, I doubted that he would, but as we all know, it's better to be safe than sorry.

I went back to the galley and met up with the purser. I asked him about the hijacker on the floor.

– Severely wounded, but alive, he said. Should come under medical care as soon as possible. I have tried to stop his bleeding and I hope that was sufficient.

He looked at me as though he wanted confirmation that he had done the right thing, and I nodded and tried to look appreciative. I actually was appreciative, it's just that I don't know if I was able to show it.

I gave the last cable tie to the purser, pointed at the seemingly lifeless body on the floor and said something like "If, if".

Still in the presence of the purser I let out a sigh of relief. I closed my eyes for a couple of seconds and said:

– We did it! It's over. Soon we'll land in Windhoek, and the police and the paramedics will take care of the hijackers. Please, inform the pilots that the situation they might not be aware of, is sorted and that we have everything under control. And ask them to inform Air Traffic Control that we would need police and medical assistance standing by when we land.

I felt elated, almost ecstatically exhilarated. We had experienced an exceptional ordeal, but almost against all odds, we had finally succeeded to overcome the obstacles, and brought the situation to a satisfactory ending. Well done us!

I smiled and looked at the purser. He stared at me with his eyes wide open, but the joy and the elated smile was missing. Instead, he looked just as worried as ever before.

I was soon about to find out why.

Chapter 4

I looked at the purser's troubled face, and suddenly felt the need to check the time. My watch said that we should have landed in Windhoek fifteen minutes ago. I wanted to ask the purser if he knew why we hadn't landed yet, but something in the look on his face said that he was actually about to tell me.

– There is a third hijacker in the cockpit, he said. One of the hijackers forced his way into the cockpit when Gaia was about to deliver coffee to the pilots.

He looked at one of the flight attendants. I glanced at her and she looked back, scared as though she was afraid that I would accuse her of something. I wasn't. I nodded at her, hopefully comforting. I don't know if I succeeded in conveying any comfort at this point. Honestly, I don't think I had any comfort left to convey…

– But we are landing in Windhoek? I asked, slowly realising that the fact that we hadn't already landed indicated that Windhoek was not the intended destination of the hijackers. Of course, it wasn't!! Who hijacks a plane and orders it to fly to its scheduled destination?! It's just people like me, who are not in the hijacking business who fail to realise something as obvious as that.

– I overheard the shouting from the cockpit, said the purser. I couldn't quite hear where the hijackers wanted to go, but the captain shouted that it was too far, and that we didn't have enough fuel to get there. Then there was a bang, and then I heard no more sounds. I'm afraid that the hijacker has taken over the cockpit, and now he is taking us towards a destination we cannot reach because we don't have enough fuel.

This was enough information to completely obliterate the tiniest residue of my previous good moods. The third hijacker must have been the third man I saw standing outside the lavatory in the front, when this whole thing started. The commotion I thought I heard was probably when the hijacker forced his way into the cockpit, and the voices thereafter would have been the heated arguments between the captain and the hijacker. The fact that we hadn't already landed was an indication of who had won.

I needed a moment to process this new piece of information. I needed a break, I needed to rest. But then again, how much time did we actually have? Neither one of us knew for how long we could stay in the air on the fuel the plane was carrying. What was this guy thinking? There was no reason to doubt the captain when he said that there was not enough fuel to reach the hijackers' desired destination. So, what was the hijackers' plan and what could we possibly do in this situation to stop it?

If there was anything we actually could do, it had to be done in the cockpit, this much was clear. The purser looked at me and I looked at him. That didn't help, of course, but at least it confirmed a sort of comradery, which in reality was established even before.

My brain rebooted, and returned to my initial thoughts when I was first made aware of the hijacking:

1. We are all going to die.

   Actually, that was at this point confirmed, given the stupidity of a hijacker attempting to fly the plane towards a destination not possible to reach with the available amount of fuel.

2. Is there anything I can do for anyone else on the plane during these last few moments?

   Well, giving up my window seat to the young girl, helping the Frenchman (or whatever nationality he was), freeing the cabin crew and making the purser feel less alone, had to do at this point.

3. What can I do to make it as difficult as possible for the hijackers to do us harm?

   That was the question which needed to be addressed at this point.

– Is there a way to enter the cockpit? I asked.

To answer this question, the purser gave a long, thorough and detailed explanation of how the cockpit door lock works, with keypad and switches and other different prerequisites for being able to enter the cockpit from the cabin. He pointed at a red light lit at the keypad, indicating that the door was locked from inside the cockpit.

– Unless the door is unlocked from inside the cockpit, there is no way of getting in. In the case it remains locked we would have to break down the door, and we have no tools to do that, the purser said.

I was painfully aware of the fact that the only tool we had access to, was the purser's tiny screwdriver, and the magnitude of the problem we were facing became more and more clear, not to say; overwhelming. I wanted to sit down. I wanted to rest. I wanted to return to my seat in row 20, while mumbling to myself "Sod it. I don't bloody care anymore!" And I just wanted to sit there and close my eyes and wait for the inevitable to happen. I wanted to submerge myself in the pool of self-pity and indifference! That's what I wanted to do.

So, the only possible way to enter the cockpit was to trick the hijacker to unlock it. I could not come up with any other idea, and no one had at this point presented anything different, either. All this was of course under the assumption that the hijacker was presently the one in charge in the cockpit, but there was nothing to contradict this assumption.

– If the hijackers in the cabin want to speak to the one in the cockpit, could they use the intercom? I asked.

– The interphone is broken, the purser said.

He looked at me as if he wondered whether I thought he should feel good or bad about that.

Together with the question of how to get access to the cockpit was for me still the all-important question of; why me? Why should I take responsibility for the progress in this situation? I knew that even if the situation had been serious up till now, it was definitely going to be much more serious if we continued. Getting into the cockpit and taking on a hijacker who probably already killed or seriously harmed the pilots in there, was definitely nothing I wanted to do.

I looked around. Some of the other passengers had now come up to us at the front but they kept a respectful (or was it a fearful) distance. I looked at their faces. They all looked at me and the purser. The question in their faces was – What now?

Well, there were two main possibilities:

1. We would not be able to pass the cockpit door.
2. The information we had at this point gave us no other option in that case, than to wait for the engines to flame out, first one and then the other. After that, a rather short period of silent gliding, which would feel like the major part of an eternity, and then the big crash which presumably none of us would survive. Or:
3. We would be able to pass the cockpit door.
4. This would open up a number of possibilities, of which the majority were, to be honest, not the best. But then again, the others were also not the worst.

Back to the question; How to trick the hijacker to unlock the door? We could assume that the hijacker in the cockpit was ignorant of what had been going on in the cabin. We could cling to the hope that he was under the assumption that his companions had everything under control. The fact that the interphone was broken was actually something that worked in our favour. This meant that the hijacker in the cockpit never could expect the others to use the phone to speak to him, nor could he himself call the hijackers in the cabin.

We could also assume (or maybe rather hope) that the hijackers in the cabin were not trained cabin crew. This in turn would mean that they would not be familiar with the different ways of communicating with, or getting access to, the cockpit.

The cockpit door could be opened by the cabin crew with an access code from the keypad, if the pilots had unlocked it from the cockpit. This would mean that if we could in any way confirm the belief of the hijacker in the cockpit, that everything was going according to plan in the cabin, but that the cabin hijackers needed to speak to the one in the cockpit, the door would be unlocked. How to do that?

One way was, of course, to knock gently on the door and try to impersonate one of the cabin hijackers. The problem for me was that I couldn't. I hadn't heard the voice of the hijacker who spoke, enough to be able to imitate him and also, he spoke a language I couldn't speak. Could anyone else? I looked around, and just looking at their faces I could tell that no one was eager to make a try. Furthermore, we only had one chance. If the hijacker in the cockpit were to have even the slightest doubt of the authenticity of the voice, he would not unlock the door.

I turned to the purser:

– What if you would sound like you're being tortured and forced to give up the code, I asked. You would have to scream so it would be heard through the door, and you would have to make it sound real and believable.

He looked at me. I could see his brain working. He was processing the idea and working out a plan of his own. Finally, he nodded.

– When? he said.

– Let's plan this thoroughly, I said. You scream and give out the code, and when he unlocks the door, you press the code and I immediately open it and enter. I would need people behind me to back me up for whatever awaits me inside.

When I said that, I could see some of the passengers taking a step back. So much for back up! So, what did I have?

Well, I had the weapon I had taken from the hijacker on the cabin floor. Presumably it worked for one bullet. That was my hope and everything I had to cling to. Apart from that, I had nothing. The hijacker had presumably emptied his weapon against one of the pilots. That was a plausible explanation to the bang that the crew members had heard before the cockpit went silent. Did he have more than one weapon or was it probable that they just had smuggled on board one weapon each? This was anyone's guess, but again, my only hope.

In the middle of these considerations, the Frenchman (or whatever nationality he was) turned up. With the help of some other passengers apparently the situation in the back of the cabin had stabilised to the extent that he was able to leave and come to the front of the cabin to check what was going on. I was relieved and happy to see him. He was definitely better suited than anyone else on the plane to take on the hijacker in the cockpit. I looked at him and gave him a nod to greet him and welcome him to the party. I pointed at him and at the still locked cockpit door with my face making it a question. He nodded. I felt even more relieved. He would be in the frontline and take on the hijacker in the cockpit. I took out the weapon which I had put in the side pocket of my cargo trousers. I was just about to hand it to him, and explain the trigger mechanism on the side of it when the purser began his performance.

And what a performance! Standing in front of the door to the cockpit, halfway turned towards it, he started to make loud noises. "No!" he cried. "No… Please… no!!" "No, I can't…I don't have it!!! I won't give it to you!!!" "Aouw… Aouw… Please!!!" His voice kept getting louder and louder. I was mesmerised. His voice conveyed at the same time tremendous pain and futile resistance. I saw the other passengers backing away staring at him with eyes and mouths wide open. Some of the passengers in the front rows were covering their faces while others were covering their ears. This was the real deal. This was, at least as far as I at that moment could judge, an award-winning performance. I was just in the middle of hoping that the Frenchman (or whatever nationality he was) would take this opportunity to learn a thing or two about acting, when suddenly there was some sort of commotion in the back of the cabin and he took off, apparently having to deal with it.

The purser cried and whimpered like a broken man. In a high-pitched voice, he cried out: "Seven… three… seven… seven… zero… zero!" The last digits were accompanied by a loud sobbing and screams of despair and desperation. Boy, he really went all in. But 737-700?! Really!?! The model number of the aircraft! A child could have… But then I reminded myself of the fact that I hadn't, so I guess it actually worked as a secret number. But still, seriously…

The red light on the keypad was suddenly turned off. The hijacker had unlocked the door. However, the Frenchman (or whatever nationality he was) had returned to the back of the cabin to secure the situation there, and I still had the weapon in my hand. There was no turning back now. It was now or never and the only shot (literally) we had.

I nodded at the purser and he punched in the numbers on the keypad. There was a click at the door and this was it. I had to open the door. I didn't want to. I really didn't want to. I could only imagine what I would be faced with on the other side of the door, and my imagination didn't do me any favours at this point. Every part of me protested, asking for somebody else to do it. But there was no one else. *I* had to do it. So, I did. When the door opened, I saw the captain and the blood on the floor, I also saw the First Officer slumped in his seat. The hijacker, sitting in the left seat, the captain's seat, had turned his head and caught sight of me. This was not the sight he was expecting, or what he wanted for that matter. He made himself ready to face and eliminate his unwelcome intruder. He tried to get up from the seat, but had forgotten that he had strapped himself in with the seatbelt. He fell back into the seat again and used both his hands to try to unbuckle the seatbelt.

I knew I would have half a second to act. This was it. If the hijacker came free from the seatbelt and came at me, I would have nothing to match his power and skill. I would be doomed and we would all be doomed. The only advantage I had at this moment was their homemade gun which either worked, or didn't.

Well, I know almost nothing about aviation and absolutely nothing about firearms, but something tells me that firing a gun inside the cockpit of an airplane at thirty thousand feet (or any altitude, come to think of it), that is probably not a good idea. If one does that, I think it would be important to make sure that the bullet neither penetrates the skin of the aircraft, nor hits any essential flight controls or any other of the necessary gadgets.

I threw myself forward and reached the captains seat, where the hijacker had both his hands still occupied with trying to unlock himself. I held the weapon close to the top of his shoulder, next to his neck, pointed it downwards and slightly to the left, and I pressed the trigger. This one worked too. The gun went off with a loud bang, and the bullet entered the hijacker's body. He immediately slumped forward in the seat. His body was held up only by the seatbelt he had been unable to unlock.

If the situation up until now had been unreal, chaotic and frightening – at this point it had passed all conceivable limits. I now found myself in the cockpit of an airplane together with three dead bodies, of which I myself had killed one. Nothing in all my years as an accountant had prepared me for anything like this. I had once liquidated a company, but that was on the request of the owner. That was somewhat exciting at first, simply because I had never been the liquidator of a company before, but that particular excitement was soon replaced by the boring and familiar task of filling in forms and sending them to the authorities. The present situation brought excitement and stress of a level a world apart from the other.

My brain went into defence-mode and started repeating; "But it's not my fault! It's not my fault! It's not my fault! It's not my fault!" I had to make it stop. It sounded like a five-year-old or a CEO of a major company.

My hands were shaking, my head was spinning, and my legs declared unwillingness to support me. I closed my eyes and reached for something to hold on to, anything to prevent me from falling over. When I opened my eyes again, I realised that the grip my right hand had found, was the shoulder of the dead hijacker in the captain's seat.

This was when my stomach revealed the intention to make its content leave my body through any available exit, upper or lower. I needed a break. I needed a puke pause. At that moment the Frenchman (or whatever nationality he was) turned up again. I pointed at the bodies and made some gesture expressing a wish to clear the cockpit. He nodded. Not a natural conversationalist he was, but all I (or indeed anyone else, for that matter) needed at the moment.

On my way out of the cockpit, aiming for the lavatory I caught the attention of the purser. He offered me a bottle of water, which I took, and then asked him if he spoke French.

– A little, he said.

– I've asked him to remove the bodies, I said, pointing at the Frenchman (or whatever nationality he was). Please, make sure that the yoke and the column isn't touched or moved in any way, because this would disengage the autopilot.

I could see that he understood what I meant. He nodded. He was certainly willing to step up and out of his comfort zone. He understood what was needed to be done and he was willing to do it.

I set course to the lavatory. I needed a moment for myself. I had needs of body, mind and soul to attend to. This was since long, too much for me. I didn't know for how much longer I could keep standing upright.

Well inside the lavatory, I first of all took care of my bodily needs. If I would have had the strength and the mental capacity, I would have thought more about the extraordinary task I had asked the purser to perform. This was with all certainty not in the purser's work description, or manual, for that matter. If it had been in the manual, I would imagine it something like this:

Excerpts from Purser Work Manual

Section C – Extraordinary situations and tasks

Par. 241   Removing a dead, or otherwise incapacitated person from the seats in the cockpit while in flight.

- First make sure that the autopilot is engaged. This can be done by checking the control light marked A/P on the front panel.
- Make a precautionary look out the front window to make sure that the airplane is cruising at sufficient altitude to avoid involuntary contact with mountains or other ground-based objects.
- *Note: It is of utmost importance that the yoke and the column of the yoke remain untouched during the operation, to avoid disconnecting the autopilot!*
- Release the locking mechanism of the seat, and carefully slide the seat backwards, making sure that the legs or other parts of the person's body in the seat does not touch the yoke or the column. Slide the seat backwards as far as possible, and then towards the side of the cockpit (to the right on the right-hand seat, and to the left on the left-hand seat). This is to facilitate the removal of the person in the seat.
- Raise the armrest of the seat and disconnect and remove all parts of the seatbelt.
- Remove the person by inserting your arms under the arms of the person in the seat, locking your hands across the chest of the person to be removed.
- Remove the person, preferably out of the cockpit.
- After completion of the task, a brief moment of silent panic is allowed, provided that it is kept unnoticeable for other staff and/or passengers.

I don't know exactly what's wrong with me, but I sort of like writing instructions…

Nevertheless, I came to the conclusion that since we, with all certainty, were going to crash, I would prefer not to die in the lavatory with my trousers at my ankles. As a result of which, I finished my business in the lavatory, rinsed my mouth with the water from the water bottle, tried to clean up to the best of my, at this point rather reduced ability, and returned actually a little bit refreshed, to the activities outside.

The cockpit was cleared of bodies, which was a relief. On the other hand, the bodies were placed on the galley floor, which made them the first thing I saw when I came out of the lavatory. For a split second it made me want to return to the relative calm and tranquillity of the refuge I just left. Instead of returning, I took a couple of seconds to cross myself in front of the bodies. This was my way of paying tribute to the Captain and the First Officer who gave their lives in their effort to keep us safe. They deserve a proper state funeral if we get down in one piece, I thought.

Speaking of which, who flies the plane? I looked into the cockpit. Splendid – The autopilot. A steady straight line, then. At least until the fuel runs out…

I saw the purser among the passengers standing in front of the cabin.

– Is there anyone on the plane who can actually fly it, I asked.

– I'll check, he said.

Well, now is a time to do that as good as any… I thought.

While waiting for someone to step up and take over, I sat down in the left-hand seat, the captain's seat. For some reason I picked up the headset and put it on my head. I could hear a voice in the headset as I did that.

– …fied aircraft identify yourself, the voice said.

What? Was that meant for us? Again, the voice said:

– Unidentified aircraft, please ident!

Yes, that must be us. How does one operate this thing? There was a button on the yoke, and I pressed it, very careful not to disturb the yoke and thereby disconnecting the autopilot. I said:

– Mayday, mayday, mayday! This is…

Who were we? I suppressed the urge to say "My name is Karl Sandström. I'm a Swedish citizen, born and raised in the north of…" but I realised that perhaps it was not my life story the voice was after. My eyes fell on a tape attached to the dashboard (or whatever it's called in an airplane). It said V5-TZA13. I continued:

– This is Victor Five dash Tango Zulu Alpha One Three. We're an African Airline scheduled flight from Maputo to Windhoek. We have been hijacked. The hijackers are dead or incapacitated, but both pilots are dead.

Silence. Probably stunned, but silence all the same. After a short while:

– Mayday acknowledged. Confirm you have been hijacked.

– Affirmative. (Apparently, I've picked up some useful terminology, as well as what is known as the NATO alphabet, from watching Air Crash Investigation.)

– But the hijackers are no longer in charge, I continued. (Let's make it simple for the poor Air Traffic Controller.)

At this point the purser came back from his quest and tapped on my shoulder. When I looked up at him, he shook his head with a worried face. Oh no! If we actually would have had a plan, this was not going according to it. I resumed my conversation with the ATC:

– My name is Karl. I'm a passenger on this flight. I have no experience of flying an aircraft whatsoever. I'm in the cockpit of a Boeing 737-700. Is there anyone with you that has pilot experience from a 737 or similar aircraft?

– Negative. Please change your squawk code to seven seven zero zero and change radio frequency to one two one decimal five.

This would probably be a piece of cake for someone who knew how to change the squeak code and how to operate (or even how to find) the radio. I looked around. I was surrounded by knobs and buttons and switches and gadgets and thingamabobs with letters meant to describe their functions, which I couldn't interpret or understand. I was completely lost. And alone.

– Please also give the number of souls on board, amount of fuel remaining and state your intention, the voice said.

I wanted to press the button on the yoke and scream into the microphone "Please understand that you are talking to someone who doesn't know anything about flying, and doesn't understand what you're saying!!"

I didn't. Instead, I pressed the button and said:

– Please wait.

I turned to the purser who was still standing behind me in the cockpit:

– Please ask the flight attendants to go down the aisle and address every single passenger, and ask them if anyone has the slightest knowledge of flying. Any type of airplane, or know anything at all about flying. Just anything.

He nodded and went to pass on the order to the rest of the cabin crew.

Not at any point did I envy the flight attendants who had the ungrateful task of running up and down the aisle to comfort the anxious passengers with words like: "Don't worry, everything is under control. We will be landing soon, and we will announce that shortly. Just in case it will be a rough landing, we would want you to assume and maintain brace position, but we will announce that as soon this is about to happen. But, don't worry, it's all under control." And now they had the even more ungrateful task of asking the passengers if anyone knew how to fly the plane!

I sat back in the seat which apparently now was my seat. I closed my eyes. This was just too much. It was beyond me. I couldn't do this. I couldn't cope with this. This was it. We were actually all going to die, and with me at the wheel (or actually at the yoke), no less. OK, I was back in the Indian Ocean prepared to drown. For no good reason, I recapitulated our situation: First we started off with two qualified pilots flying the plane. Then we had one malicious person who possibly could fly the plane, but stubbornly wanted to take it to a destination impossible to reach. Now, because of me, we had no one who could actually fly the plane. What a splendid development! If only there had been anyone on the ground who could help me, but ATC had no one, and I had no one.

Unless, of course, my son-in-law! In my excited, confused and overwhelmed state, I had forgotten about him. Maybe he could do something for me. He was a real pilot, now working for a major airline as a First Officer on another type of airplane, but I remembered that in his previous employment he was actually flying B737s. He was stationed abroad, and unfortunately, I didn't have his phone number, and the phone wouldn't work anyway at this altitude, or was it? But I did have him on WhatsApp. Could there be Wi-Fi on this plane? Some airlines actually offered that as a treat to their passengers. But this airline?

The purser had re-joined me in the cockpit after sending the flight attendants off on their mission. I asked him:

– Is there Wi-Fi on this plane?

– Yes, we just installed it! He said it with unconcealed pride. It costs 7 dollars per…

I didn't have to look at him. And when I turned around to do so, he looked terribly embarrassed.

– I will turn it on for you sir, he said, and hurried out of the cockpit.

He returned a few moments later.

– There is a password you will have to enter, he said.

I took out my phone, unlocked it, opened the Wi-Fi settings and gave it to him. My phone was set in Swedish, of course, but that would probably not be any problem for him. I trusted that a man carrying a mini screwdriver in the inside pocket of his jacket, should know his way around electronic gadgets of different sorts. He punched in the code and handed the phone back to me.

– There you go. You now have internet access.

As I was about to open WhatsApp on my phone, the flight attendant, who I now know was named Gaia, appeared in the cockpit door together with a young girl. Gaia looked at the purser, who nodded, and then she turned to me and said:

– This is Alicia. She says she has had a few flying lessons at a flight school in Maputo. She's the only one that…

I looked at Alicia. This was a young girl. She could be twenty, at most. She looked terrified, and all of her appearance said "Why did I say that? Why did I admit to anything? Forget this, I want to go back to my seat!" I tried to give her a confident smile, and she tried to smile back at me. She didn't succeed either. She must have seen the bodies of the dead pilots in the galley on her way to the cockpit, and that must have scared her out of her wits.

– So, you've had some flying lessons, I said.

– I haven't done my solo yet, she said. I'm supposed to do that next time…

She turned away towards the cabin as if she attempted to return to her seat. I didn't want to force her, but then again, I needed all the help I could get. We all did.

– Thanks for stepping up, I said. Your help is very much needed and greatly appreciated.

– I… I don't know how much help I can be, she said.

Her voice was trembling. She definitely didn't think that she belonged in the cockpit. Well, I definitely didn't think I belonged in the cockpit either, so welcome, you'll fit right in!

– I'm Karl, by the way, I said.

– Alicia, said Alicia.

– Listen, I don't want to scare you, I said, but I have to inform you of the situation. The pilots are no longer with us, and the hijacker who could fly the plane is dead. He tried to take us towards a destination that would be impossible to reach because there simply isn't enough fuel. The captain explained that before he was ki… Anyway, I'm just a passenger who don't know (I was about to say "anything" but changed it to) much about flying. Would you like to sit in the captain's seat?

She looked absolutely terrified and just shook her head.

– Well then, if you would just please strap yourself in the co-pilot's seat and help out with anything you can possibly think of, that would be great!

I stressed the "please" part to put just a little bit of pressure on her. She looked very hesitant, but slowly made her way to the seat and started to figure out how to strap herself in. She was still shaking, obviously terrified, and I for one couldn't blame her. Oddly enough, just having her there made me feel better. I felt a little calmer, a little less alone.

– I'm about to call a friend who is a pilot, I said. He will help us sort this out. He knows the bits and bobs about the 737. He's flown these himself, not long ago.

I don't know if this information helped calm her down. She didn't say anything. But at least I suppressed my desire to shout out a joyful "Let's fly this thing!" There was no need to give her the impression that she just strapped herself in the cockpit together with a complete maniac. She would find that out for herself anyway, in due time.

I opened WhatsApp on my phone, and started to look for him. Daniel where are you? Was it that long since we last had a conversation? I scrolled down to the bottom. He was nowhere to be found. Come on, where are you? I scrolled up again, slower this time and there he was! Now I only needed him to be reachable and not flying over the Atlantic or something with his phone turned off. I pressed the Call button. After a moment I could hear it ringing. One signal.

Two signals. Three signals. Four signals. Come on! Please, please, please, God please! Five signals.

– Ahm, hrm, uh…, hello? … Karl? Is that you?

If ever I had heard someone being awaken by the phone, it was now.

– Karl, it's in the middle of the night. I'm in a hotel in New York and I'm flying back home tomorrow morning, ahm, actually today, in a couple of hours. Can this wait?

– No, I'm afraid it can't. Listen, I'm in Africa and…

– Oh, that's nice. Say hello to Africa from me…

I could hear that he was returning to sleep, happy that his father-in-law reported that he was in Africa.

Actually, I had experienced this before, with his wife, my daughter, when she was young and still lived with me. I woke her up late at night because I could smell smoke in the apartment, and I was afraid that the building was on fire. I brought her with me to the living room, and asked her if she could smell smoke as well, and she said "Yes". When I turned to look at her, she was on her way back to her room. I asked her what she was doing. "What if there is a fire?" I said. She crawled back to bed, and said something like "If there really is a fire you can wake me up then…" That's kids for you. I don't know whether to call them trusting, or just plain stupid.

– Listen Daniel! I said. I'm on a plane in Africa. We have been hijacked. The hijackers are subdued but they have killed both the pilots. I'm alone in the cockpit with a young lady who has had ten flying lessons in a Cessna. We're cruising on autopilot, but we need to get this plane full of people on the ground! ATC has no one to help us. Could you please!

I don't know if it was ten flying lessons, or if it was a Cessna, but I needed to wake him up and get his attention. There was silence in the phone. I didn't know if the connection was broken, or if he had returned to the land of dreams, or if he was slowly taking in the information given. It turned out to be the latter, sort of.

– Aha, a Cessna, he said

Okay, he was waking up, but much too slowly for our needs.

– I'm really sorry to wake you up, but there are…

I turned to the purser:

– How many souls on board?

– Ninety-seven souls and three dead.

– Ninety-seven souls on board, I said to the telephone. We're in a 737-700, cruising on autopilot. The pilots are dead and we really need your help! Would you please wake up!

– Yes, I'm awake.

His voice sounded serious. Finally, he was awake, and I had his attention.

– I've sent out a mayday and ATC has asked us to change the squeak code or was it the squeal code to seven seven zero zero and also to change the radio frequency to a number I can't remember but I can ask them again. I'll put you on speaker so everyone can hear.

I set the phone to speaker and placed it on the centre console. I checked the battery level on the phone. 53 percent. Hopefully that will last a while. Now the only thing to worry about was losing the internet connection. Apart from everything else, of course! I chuckled. When I looked up, I saw Alicia, my newly appointed co-pilot staring at me. Her eyes showed panic.

– I'm not crazy, I'm not crazy, I assured her.

– What? Said Daniel on the phone.

This was getting complicated and already a bit out of hand. It was time to steer things up. Myself mostly, as usual.

– How do I change the squeal code? I asked, addressing the telephone.

– The squawk code, said Daniel.

– The what?

– It's called the squawk code.

– Well, if you say so. Why should I change it, and how do I change it?

– The squawk code 7700 tells everyone around you that you're in trouble. You change it on the transponder at the lower part of the centre console. It's in the middle, just below the red fire extinguisher switches for the engines.

Well, if it is to inform the world around us, I guess it makes sense. Those of us who were presently in the cockpit didn't need any extra reminder that we were in trouble. We were all fully aware of this.

Alicia had paid close attention to what Daniel said, and had already found the dial. She looked up as to ask how to change it.

– And how do we change the numbers? I asked the telephone.

– There are two buttons below the window that shows the squawk code. If you turn them, the numbers in the window change. Turn them till the window says 7700, said Daniel.

Alicia was already on it, and I watched her changing the numbers. Finally, the little window showed 7700. Our dire situation was now transmitted to the outside world.

– Done. I said to the telephone. Now, the ATC wanted us to change radio frequency to a number I have forgotten. I guess I can ask them again.

– Probably 121.5, said Daniel. That's the international emergency frequency.

– Yes, that sounds like the one, I said. Do you want me to double check?

– No need, said Daniel. They might want you on another frequency, but if you transmit on the emergency, they will still be able to hear you, and they can give you instructions from there.

– Okay. So, how do we change it?

– First of all, check if the frequency is already pre-set on one of the radios. It's possible that one of the radios have the emergency frequency set as stand by. You can see the frequencies set in the displays. There are three radios. One and two are on either side of the transponder and number three is just below it. Does either radio have 121.5 on the display?

Sharp eyed Alicia found the displays and pointed at radio number two. I had a thought. Why not set the emergency frequency as stand by on the radio currently in use. That radio had the frequency used in our contact with the ATC. By setting the emergency frequency as stand by on that radio, we could make that frequency active, see if it works, and if it doesn't, we could easily switch back to the frequency previously used. There's just one rub:

– How do we know which radio is in use, I asked the telephone.

– On the centre console there is a set of buttons marked MIC SELECTOR, said Daniel. Which one is lit?

– The first from the left, I said.

– So, that's radio number one then, said Daniel.

– I'll set the emergency frequency as stand by on that one, and then make it active before trying to contact ATC.

– Yes, do that, said Daniel. By the way, which button did you use when you were transmitting?

– I found a button on the yoke, I said, but I was very careful not to make the yoke move so that the autopilot would be disconnected, because I don't know how to reactivate it.

– There is a toggle switch just below the mic selector buttons, which says R/T. It's better if you use that one instead of the one on the yoke, so you don't risk disconnecting the autopilot. By the way, if you'd accidently do that, the autopilot can be reengaged by pressing the CMD-button under A/P Engage on the front panel. Do you know exactly where you are and how much fuel you have?

– No, I have no idea where we are, or how much fuel we have, but we should have landed half an hour ago so I doubt there is much left. Is there a fuel gauge somewhere?

– On the centre screen where the engine performances are displayed, in the lower right hand side corner there is a type of fuel gauge. Try to make out what it says.

– I think it says 3.2 tons, but I'm not sure.

– Contact ATC and tell them that you are low on fuel, and that you need vectors to the nearest airport.

I toggled the R/T switch, and called ATC for the first time on the emergency frequency.

– Mayday, mayday this is Victor five. Do you read? Over.

I later found out that the number I saw written in front of me, V5-TZA13, was not our actual call-sign. Instead, it was the registration number of the aircraft. (However, being the only one currently in trouble on the emergency frequency, I could just as well introduce myself as I did when calling the local bank in the village where I grew up in the north of Sweden – "Hi, it's me again" …)

The frequency change worked, and I was relieved to hear the now familiar voice of the ATC controller:

– Reading you loud and clear. Say your intention.

– We need vectors for the nearest airport. Low on fuel.

– Your nearest airport would be Maun International Airport, that's Mike Alpha Uniform November. They can offer an ILS approach. Would you like to go there?

– Yes, please. Where exactly is that?

– It's in the northern part of Botswana. You want vectors for Maun?

– Yes, as direct as possible, please. We don't have much fuel left. I just hope that it will be enough to get us there.

I told Daniel about which airport ATC advised for landing, and it turned out that he actually had the landing charts for Maun International Airport on his iPad. It felt good to know that he knew where we were going, and what the landing situation would look like.

We received vectors for our destination, and Daniel helped us find where to set the heading, and how to make the autopilot follow the instructions. There were also a number of requests from the ATC of altitude changes, and with the help of Daniel we managed to make these changes. Everything up to this point worked smoothly, mostly because of Alicia, who listened to Air Traffic Control on one ear and to Daniel on the other ear. She was quick to find the buttons and switches, and to work out how to use them. Without her help in the cockpit, I would have been totally lost. My brain gave overload warning, and I had to be careful not to make it shut down completely. That had happened in the past, and this was not a good moment for it to happen again.

All of a sudden, I heard Daniel say:

– Is it okay if I leave you for a minute? I need to call my captain and inform her of the situation, and I need to get dressed.

My response of course was:

– No, wait! What… why? No, just keep the phone on and with you!

But it was too late. The phone had gone silent. Daniel was apparently phoning his captain to inform him (or was it her?) of our situation, and subsequently – his. I totally understood his need to inform his superior officer, as well as his need to get properly dressed for the day, it was just that the phone being silent made a scary situation even more scary. Daniel was literally our lifeline. Without him on the phone we would not stand a chance. With him, maybe we actually had a chance to make it. Could it be that we actually had a chance? I started to contemplate the idea of a positive outcome. I allowed the thought of us getting out of this situation alive, to take up space in my consciousness, and I immediately regretted it, feeling my nerves' reaction. No, if I were to have any possibility of keeping my nerves in check, the only way to look at it would be to immediately return to my original thought; we are going to crash and die. With that once again settled I eagerly awaited Daniel's return to the phone. (This made no sense, of course. If we actually were going to crash, the last thing I wanted for Daniel was for him to listen to the sound of a crash which he could do nothing about, sitting in a hotel room in New York. Having him on the phone, on the other hand, would give us a fighting chance of actually making it down in one piece. The prospect of which would make me incapacitated out of fear and nerves. I get really tired of myself sometimes.)

– I've asked the captain to come to my room.

Daniel was back on the phone. I guess he had been gone for about a minute, but it felt like forever and a half.

– Now I just need to get dressed, but that is quick, and I can stay with you on the phone while I'm putting my clothes on.

I was very grateful that he understood how important it was for us to know that he was available, even if nothing appeared to happen at our end. The plane was cruising on autopilot according to the heading, altitude and speed directions provided for us by the ATC and which by the help of Daniel were set up, but the thing with not knowing what could happen is that you don't know what might happen…

– Wait, said Daniel, I hear the captain knocking on my door. I'll just let her in.

I guess he had changed his pyjamas to a more suitable attire for his upcoming duty, as well as for receiving his captain, who apparently was a lady, but then again, that was more his problem than mine. After a moment I heard a female voice over the phone:

– Hello, my name is Captain O'Hare, the voice said. I understand that you find yourself in a tricky situation.

I acknowledged that. To me, it was difficult to imagine a situation more tricky. It was however, comforting to know that we now had not just one, but two experts on the other side of the phone. I was also glad to learn that Daniel had with him someone with whom he could share the burden. If anything went wrong with the landing, there would be someone whose professional expertise he respected, who could tell him that whatever went wrong, it was not his fault, that he was not to blame, that he had provided us with correct information and guidance, and that he had done everything in his ability and power to help us.

I could hear Daniel tell her everything he knew about our situation. I could not hear her disagreeing with anything he said.

– This is going to be just fine. Daniel tried his best to sound convincing.

He could learn a thing or two about acting from the purser, I thought to myself.

– You have landed a plane before, haven't you? He continued.

– No! Wait, what? No! No, I mean…

I guess I must have told him about the time when my family chipped in for my 60th birthday; a one-hour plane ride which gave me the opportunity to fly a plane myself, accompanied by an instructor who was a real pilot.

This was a microlight airplane, in the size of an oversized raincoat, with just enough room for two people; a single engine propeller plane named Ikarus.

I do not understand why airplane manufacturers insist of naming planes after things that cannot fly. In this case even the manufacturer is named after the character in Greek mythology, Icarus, who made himself wings from bird feathers glued together with wax. As the myth goes, Icarus was caught by hubris, and flew too high and too close to the sun, whereby the wax in his wings melted, the feathers came loose, and he plunged to his death. What a great name for an airplane…

Anyway, this took place on the west coast of Sweden, with an instructor who had been a fighter pilot in either Iraq or Iran, I can't remember which. He had flown MIG fighter jets anyway, and apparently had no problem with having an accountant making his first experience as a pilot in a propeller plane. We took off from an airfield which in the early parts of the twentieth century had been a training facility for the Swedish army – a huge grass field. After a few moments in the air, the instructor handed the control over to me. With great caution I guided the plane over places I had visited, and knew. The weather was perfect, and I had the time of my life. I was immensely enjoying myself. At one time I looked over to the instructor. I noticed that the former fighter pilot tried his best to stay awake. This was probably the most boring 60 minutes he had had in a plane in a long time.

When my allowed 60 minutes were almost up, it was time to return to the airfield. The instructor then told me that if I wanted, I could land the plane myself. I guess it was his only way of getting any kind of excitement out of an otherwise extremely boring flight. With his instructions I aimed for the airfield and succeeded to make the main gear touch the ground. Now, as I've previously made clear – I know nothing about flying, but I think I know this much; landing on the nosewheel is never a good idea. In a single engine propeller plane, landing on a grass field with an uneven surface, it might, for the non-experienced pilot, perhaps be a good thing to be a little bit careful. "Nose down", said the fighter pilot. I gently pushed the control-stick forward, but apparently not aggressively enough for the instructor. "Nose down!" he repeated. It became obvious that my gentle touch on the control-stick was not to his satisfaction, and he grabbed the stick which was situated between our seats, and pushed the nose down to complete the landing.

I immediately let go of the control-stick, causing him to burst out laughing. As I said, I don't know much about flying, but I don't think that two grown men fighting over the controls in a plane during landing is a good thing, especially when one is a licensed pilot and the other a visitor in a cockpit for the first time. Anyway, I was glad that I could offer him, if not excitement, at least some amusement…

In reality, I was a bit disappointed that I was prevented from completing the landing. He had his family waiting for him at the hangar to go home, and he was of course eager to finish as quickly as possible, but the field was very, very long. It would have delayed him not more than a couple of minutes to let me complete the landing in my time and cautious manner. But then again, my 60 minutes were up, and he wanted to go home with his family, and who was I to argue with that.

That was then, and this is now, but landing a commercial jetliner with more than 90 souls on board, is definitely not the same as landing a microlight plane, which can land, if not on a coin, at least on an average-size banknote.

We were now getting closer to the airport of Maun, and it was time to configure the airplane for landing. Apparently, the plane should be able to land more or less by itself, given the correct instructions. Air Traffic Control provided us with frequencies needed for the auto-land, and Daniel helped us set the autopilot and the navigation radios up so that the plane could intercept the ILS-signals from the airport. So, there was again a lot of button-pressing and knob-turning to set everything up correctly.

Daniel gave us instructions on how to set the flaps, arm the speed-brakes, and continuously with the help of Alicia, controlled the airspeed.

Suddenly the phone gave off a sound to alert us of the fact that its battery level was critically low. Disturbing news as it was, I still chose to ignore it. There were so many things which could go wrong, that one more sort of got lost in the total amount of problems, current or potential. Besides, there was not much I could do about it. I was fully occupied with more urgent matters, and I simply did not have the capacity do deal with yet another problem.

Eventually, the autopilot found the signals from the Instrument Landing System, the ILS, and the plane made its final turns towards the runway.

– I'm handing you over to the tower, the ATC voice said. They have instructions for emergency vehicles, medical assistance and police. Good luck!

A female voice, presenting herself as Maun tower, came over the radio.

– Mayday acknowledged. Emergency vehicles, medical and police are standing by, she said. You have priority and are clear to land on runway two six. Wind calm and runway dry. Report when established on glideslope and when runway in sight.

The weather was absolutely perfect for us; no clouds, no wind and a dry runway. Although, a heavy rain would have helped with the fight against the post-crash fire, I thought. But then again, you can't have everything, I suppose. I found new comfort in knowing that fire-trucks were waiting at the airport, and finally I let go of the soothing thought of imminent death, and gave the landing preparations my undivided attention.

The plane was acting on its own, so I assumed it had caught the glideslope, and we could see the runway in front of us.

– Established on glideslope and runway in sight, I reported to the tower.

– Cleared to land on runway two six, was the reply.

– Prepare the cabin for an emergency landing!! I suddenly remembered to shout, hoping that someone from the cabin crew would hear me through the still open cockpit door. This was all I could do at this moment. I had to concentrate on the landing. Hopefully their professional training would kick in. If they had heard me, that is…

Daniel asked about our speed, and gave the final instructions for landing:

– You are still a bit fast. Reduce thrust, set automatic braking to level three. When you touch down you keep the plane on the centreline with the rudder pedals. Put your feet on the pedals to be prepared, but be careful not to move them before landing. After touchdown, when nose gear is on the runway, remember what I said about the thrust reversers, although I don't think you would need them. Runway is long and dry and the automatic brakes will do the braking for you. Flaps forty, and gear down.

Alicia took care of setting the flaps and lowering the landing gear. As soon as the landing gear lights went from red to green, I reported to Daniel:

– Three green. Gear down and locked.

Alicia now turned the switch for the autobrakes to level three. As soon as she did that, a loud warning sounded in the cockpit and red warning lights lit up on the control panel. The sound was loud and immediately overheard by Daniel over the phone.

– What's happening! He shouted.

– I don't know! I answered. Something must be wrong, but I don't know what.

Daniel had identified the sound as a Master Caution Warning, and asked me to search the main display to try to find the reason why the alarm was triggered.

– It says "Autobrake". Maybe that's what's not working, I said.

– Turn the Autobrake switch back to OFF, said Daniel.

Alicia followed his instruction, and luckily the sound and lights of warning disappeared.

– You'll have to brake manually, he said. The brake pedals are just above the rudder pedals.

I could hear the tension in his voice. I guess you regret putting on a new shirt now, don't you, I thought to myself. Not that this actually was any of my concerns at this moment… (I really need to stop engaging myself in other people's problems! Especially when my own are more than I can handle.)

To make the situation even more interesting, the telephone gave us a new reminder of its battery situation. Sometimes you have no other option than to hope and pray. Since that was my only option at this point, that was the option I went with.

I could hear Captain O'Hare ask about our speed. In the stressful situation in the cockpit, as well as in the hotel room in New York, no one had paid proper attention to the airspeed. Daniel immediately relayed the question.

– 165 knots, said Alicia.

– This is way too fast, said Daniel. Thrust to idle!

Alicia put the thrust levers all the way down to idle, but we were now very close to the runway and about to land. The automatic voice heard in the cockpit started to count down, measuring our altitude over ground in feet. "50" it said, followed by "40".

– In case of a go around… said Daniel.

– No, no, no, no, no! I said. No go around. There is no way we could manage that! This is it. It's now or never.

This was rather obvious to me, and I guess Daniel and his captain also realised this.

The voice continued its relentless count-down: "30" – "20" – "10".

The plane was guided by the ILS-system to a perfect touchdown. The main gear hit the runway with the familiar thump, followed by a rattling and shaking of the aircraft indicating a slightly uneven surface. As soon as the nose gear had touched down, Alicia and I stamped on the brakes, both of us using all of our strength. Since the speed-brakes were armed, the ground-spoilers were automatically deployed as soon as there was weight on the main gear, but the plane was much too fast and eating up the runway in a very fast pace.

Everything was now happening very quickly, and the stress of the situation was immense. This meant that there was something that Alicia or I should have done, but which we both forgot; We both forgot to apply the thrust reversers. We were just too occupied with trying to manually brake the plane. The thrust reversers would have done the job, but with the end of the runway coming closer and closer, we just stamped on the brakes as hard as we could. Maybe a little too hard, as it turned out. Suddenly, I could feel the plane starting to skid. Apparently, in our attempt to stop the plane with the manual braking, we had pushed the brakes too hard, and thereby locked the wheels on the main gear. We were about to leave the runway and proceed out onto the grass area beside.

We were still moving much too fast, and my personal experience told me that if we would have veered off the runway and onto the grass, our possibility of stopping the plane would be substantially reduced. I will not divulge the details of my experience in the matter, let me just say that my dad's car was fully insured, and no one was seriously hurt, perhaps with the exception of my young and fragile ego.

– Ease up on the brakes! I shouted to Alicia.

I was pressing the brake pedals while trying to keep the plane on the runway with the help of the rudder pedals. My level of ambition regarding steering the plane was perhaps not to hit the centreline of the runway, but more of keeping the plane close enough to the airport facilities so that the emergency vehicles would be able to find us and reach us when we stopped. But against all odds, I actually managed to keep the plane on the runway.

The end of the runway came closer and closer, but we were also slowing down, and finally, we stopped. On the runway, no less. Incredible! I looked at Alicia and she looked at me. I guess both our eyes showed amazement and disbelief. Neither one of us said anything.

– We've stopped on the runway, I said to the telephone.

– Really? Said Daniel. One could hear the surprise and relief in his voice too.

– Congratulations! said Captain O'Hare. Well done!

I felt indescribably relieved.

– How do we turn off the engines? I asked.

– There are two kill switches below the throttle levers, Daniel said. Pull them down. That will shut the engines off. And there is a parking brake lever on the left-hand side of the centre pedestal. It says Parking brake…

As we were speaking, I could hear engine number one, the engine on the left-hand side, spool down. We were out of fuel. So much for the option of a go around. Even if someone would have had the skill and knowledge to do a go around, it wouldn't have been possible. There just wasn't enough fuel.

I didn't bother to tell Daniel at this moment. I pulled the two kill switches for the engines, heard engine number two spool down, and the engine sound died away, and I pulled the parking brake lever. We had made it! In my state of euphoria, I said:

– Maybe I should call my children to tell them I'm okay…

– Is anyone of them aware of your situation? asked Daniel.

– No… no they're not. No, you're right. I'll phone them when I get home.

– NO! That's not what I meant! Listen, we are fifteen minutes late for leaving to the airport. I'm actually flying the first leg. We have to go. Are you sure you're alright?

– Yes, very much so. Thank you so much! And thank you also, Captain, I said to the telephone. When you fly back, know that you've saved 97 souls on a flight in Africa. God's speed to you both!

As I was speaking, I could hear the telephone again giving air to a complaint concerning low battery level. Apparently, this time enough was enough, and it had decided to shut down. Hopefully Daniel and his captain had heard enough to understand how grateful I was for what they had done.

I leaned back in the seat, exhausted beyond belief. I closed my eyes for a couple of seconds, safe in the knowledge that the police and medical were on their way. I had noticed the emergency vehicles, the ambulances and the police cars close to the runway as we landed. We were safe. What could possibly go wrong now?

Chapter 5

My rest in the seat, well-earned as it may have been, didn't last long, however.

I was slowly made aware of noises coming from the cabin. There was something going on back there. I found myself forced to leave my state of total relaxation. What was happening? I became more and more agitated. I would not let anything interfere now! Absolutely not! I unbuckled the seatbelt and made my way out of the cockpit. The purser was shouting in the PA-system: "Please remain seated until the seatbelt sign has been switched off!" My brain found the time to point out to me that this could take a while, since I didn't know where to find the switch to the seatbelt signs… The flight attendants were also trying their best to make the passengers return to their seats, but to no avail. Men, women and children were all anxious and trying to get out and off as soon as possible. I for one, could not blame them. We had all been in a life-threatening ordeal and we were now safe on the ground, and they were not prepared to have anyone trying to stop them.

I put my sympathies aside as I felt a fury coming over me, from I don't know where. I ignored using the PA-system and yelled at the top of my lungs:

– SIT DOWN!! THE POLICE AND THE PARAMEDICS MUST DO THEIR JOB FIRST, BEFORE ANYONE CAN LEAVE THE PLANE! SIT DOWN!!

I went down the aisle addressing every person in the aisle who was reaching for the overhead lockers to retrieve their hand-luggage, or anyone just standing in the aisle, or even those who were just trying to get out of their seats. I shouted in their faces "SIT DOWN!" making my way down the aisle, row by row. The flight attendants followed behind me trying their best to make sure that no one resumed their effort to step out into the aisle. I was, at the same time, very careful not to touch anyone. I kept my hands behind my back, because I knew that with all the emotions and adrenalin flying around, if I had touched anyone it could have triggered a fight, in which case I would have lost in more ways than one. This was a battle I was determined not to lose. I would not have anyone interfere with the successful outcome we were all now a part of! I felt sympathy with them all, but I was determined to have this ordeal to end in an orderly and safe manner for everyone. My concerns were not the least towards the deadly wounded hijacker still lying in his blood on the aisle floor.

When I came to the rear of the cabin, I turned around. Everyone was now in their seats. Most of them at the edge of their seats, but nevertheless. In the relative silence in the cabin, I could hear banging and knocking on the cabin door. Apparently, the ground crew had managed to take a stair to the plane on the runway, and someone was now asking to be let in. I saw the purser at the front of the cabin and made a sign to him to open the door. In my excited and overambitious wish to have nothing go wrong at this stage I shouted:

– Disarm door!

I don't know why I did that. It was clearly insulting to a trained professional. That was his job, and I immediately regretted it. I must remember to apologise, I thought to myself. It's just that if he for any reason would have forgotten to disarm the door, the inflatable emergency slide would have automatically been activated and that would not only have made it very difficult for anyone from the outside to enter the plane, it could also have knocked over the stair outside and seriously injured people on the stair and/or people on the ground. Not to mention made disembarkation much more difficult.

The purser however, showed no obvious sign of disapproval. He disarmed the door and opened it.

The first persons to enter the plane were the police.

At this point I must take a moment to express my gratitude for this being Africa. Had this taken place in Europe or North America, the first persons entering the plane would have been some sort of SWAT team. Probably ten to twenty fully equipped, and fully armed, highly trained officers with helmets, bullet proof vests and automatic weapons loaded with live ammunition. All dressed in black, and all regarding each and every one on the plane as a possible perpetrator. Every passenger and crewmember would have been shouted at and threatened with guns, possibly even handcuffed, making this scene much more frightening and traumatising than the ordeal we just escaped.

This was Africa, and I was immensely grateful for the practical and almost laid-back approach from this part of the Botswanan police force.

There were five police officers entering the plane, of which one apparently was in charge of the other four. This was a man who appeared to be proud to be a police officer, he was also proud to be in charge, but he was most of all proud of his impeccable uniform. From the stripes on his perfectly maintained uniform jacket, I drew the conclusion that he was a police captain or similar.

His eyes searched the plane. He was obviously looking for someone in charge, someone with assigned authority who could inform him of the situation and explain where police assistance would be needed. His eyes found the purser. This was the only living male figure in uniform he could see. Subsequently it was the purser who had the police captain's full and undivided attention.

By this time, I had returned to the front of the cabin. I'm sorry to say, but I am Swedish. Sometimes, much too Swedish. It has from time to time caused me to end up in awkward situations, simply because I've not considered the culture of the people I was interacting with. This time was no exception. Disregarding standard protocol, I went straight to the point and blurted out what needed to be done. Without properly introducing myself, I said:

– First of all, the wounded man on the aisle floor needs immediate medical attention.

I pointed at the body lying face down on the aisle floor. The pointing was probably an automatic reflex of mine, because no one, except for the purser, paid any attention to me. The purser looked at me and the police captain looked at the purser, who was showing signs of becoming more and more uneasy. The police chief took a quick and disapproving glance at me. It was obvious that my khaki-coloured cargo trousers with matching shirt was not to his liking. In his opinion this was not how you should dress if you wanted to be taken seriously. I admit that the shirt was bought on sale for a very reasonable price, but still… Finally, in a low voice, and looking utterly embarrassed, the purser said:

– That man needs medical attention. He pointed at the wounded hijacker.

The police captain nodded. He looked satisfied. Finally, he was informed by someone with the appropriate sign of authority – a uniform. He told two paramedics to enter. They carried with them a stretcher and immediately attended to the wounded man. They turned him over, gave him oxygen, and did what else I guess paramedics do in a situation like this.

– Please, try to keep him alive, I said.

One of them looked at me as if to say "What do you think, we're doing?!" Again, my comment was perceived as trying to interfere with the expertise of trained professionals, but my remark was made for my own sake, and never meant to be a way for me to tell them how to do their job.

As they laid the wounded man on the stretcher and started to carry him out of the plane, the police captain commanded two of the officers to follow them and guard the hijacker.

As soon as the paramedics had left, Gaia turned up with a bag containing some sort of absorbing material, which she spread on the aisle floor to absorb the blood from the hijacker. This bag of whatever it was, probably was intended for other types of liquid, but worked very well also in this use. Since Gaia spread the total content of the bag over the pool of blood, it was now safe for everyone to disembark through the aisle without getting blood on their shoes.

Next item on the list was of course the captured hijacker in the rear of the cabin.

– There is a captured hijacker in the back, I said, again pointing, now to the group of men guarding the captive.

And, as before, this was totally ignored by the police captain. He had his eyes glued to the purser, who yet again, looked embarrassed, and with a low voice said:

– One of the hijackers is captured and alive at the rear of the cabin. He pointed towards the men in the back.

The police captain ordered his two remaining men to arrest the second hijacker, which they immediately carried out.

Now, the only thing left on the list was the bodies in the galley. This must have been self-explanatory to the police captain, and needed no further explanation from the purser or myself. The purser just pointed to the galley, and the captain ordered the remaining paramedics, still waiting outside, to remove the bodies from the plane.

After this was done, it was time to let everyone leave the plane. I suggested this to the purser. He nodded in agreement and made the announcement over the PA-system. This time the passengers acted much more calm and much more silent, and may I say, in a much more orderly and respectful manner.

I placed myself outside the cockpit, by the exit. I was joined by Alicia who stood there beside me. The purser and the flight attendants also positioned themselves at the front of the cabin.

I looked at Alicia. No honestly, I stared at her. What a transformation! When she entered the cockpit, she was a young girl, absolutely terrified of what may lie ahead of her, but she nevertheless stepped up, and took the responsibility placed on her by me and the situation itself. Now she was standing there, straight in the back with her head held high, apparently much aware of what she had achieved and accomplished. She was no longer a child; she was now a young woman. She knew what she had done, and what she was capable of. My heart was overflowing with pride and joy on her behalf. I wanted to express to her how I felt about her amazing achievement. I needed to tell her that none of this positive outcome of the horrendous situation we had been faced with, had been possible without her, and without her help.

– Please understand, I said to her, that what you've done has saved the plane and us. There is no way in which we could have done this without your…

I was interrupted by the passengers coming up to us and to the exit. Some of them were shaking our hands in order, from the flight attendants to the purser, to Alicia, to me. I even received a couple of kisses on the cheeks. Their gratitude was unmistakable. Words of gratitude were spoken, many of which in languages I couldn't understand, but their eyes and their smiles said it all. Most of the passengers however, were too focused to get out of the plane to even notice our existence. They had their eyes fixated on the door to freedom and could not wait another second to get off the plane after this near-death experience. The people to whom I had shouted in their faces to get back into their seats, pushed everyone else aside to get out as quickly as possible. They wouldn't even look at me, apparently not wanting to have anything to do with the Nazi in the cockpit. I couldn't blame them. I could understand their frustration and anxiety. Quite frankly, I wasn't too sad to see them leave either.

The last person of the passengers ready to leave, was the Frenchman (or whatever nationality he was). He came up to me, looked me in the eyes and stretched out his hand, but said nothing. I grabbed his hand, and the only word in French I could muster at that moment was "Merci". He nodded and went out the cabin door and down the stair. When he was halfway down the stair, I turned towards his back and said:

– Excusez-moi ! Je voudrai bien savoir lequel natio-nalité… ?

He didn't stop to turn his head. He didn't slow his pace. He just kept walking as if he hadn't heard me, which he must have done. I remember thinking to myself that whenever I tell this story in the future, he will always be named "the Frenchman (or whatever nationality he was)"…

I was later told that this was the last time anyone related to these events ever saw him. Apparently, he didn't show up at the arrival hall and left no trace of where he went. He just disappeared. As it turned out, no one could even find out who he was, where he was going or what the purpose of his trip was. I was told that he booked the flight under a false name and boarded the plane using a fake passport. No one from the police was able to find any information about him. Well, whoever he was, he is a hero in my books anyway. Nothing that happened would have happened the way it did, if it hadn't been for him. Whoever you are, wherever you are – I salute you!

The five of us were now the only persons left on the plane. It was time for us to leave, as well as saying goodbye to each other. There is a special bond created between people who have been through an ordeal like this together. Everyone gets an appreciation for everyone else, what they have contributed with, and for their person as such. Even though we knew that there were people on the tarmac waiting for us, we took the time to thoroughly thank each other and try to give words to what we were feeling. We had earned that time. The others could wait. I finally got the chance to express my sincere gratitude for Alicia and what she had done. I told her that we wouldn't have made it if it weren't for her, that I would have been lost in the cockpit on my own, and also that she never should allow anyone to diminish what she had accomplished today.

I also made my feelings of gratitude known to the purser, who went far beyond both his comfort zone as well as any job description. It was also important to let the flight attendants know that they had been likewise invaluable in this highly stressful situation. They were well trained and had acted professionally during this whole ordeal. What a fantastic cabin crew! I really hope that they will receive recognition from the airline for what they have done and endured, as well as professional counselling to help them overcome the trauma they inevitably must have suffered.

All in all, a happy group of people all thanking each other and collectively rejoicing in the fact that we after all came out of it alive, and at least physically unharmed.

I thought that this could be the last we saw of each other, so it was actually sad to prepare to leave the plane. I asked the purser and the flight attendants if it was okay with them to leave before Alicia and myself. It would have been the purser's right to leave as the last person. Since both pilots were dead, the plane and the passengers were now his responsibility. I was very touched and grateful that he was kind enough to accept. He must have waived his right as a token of appreciation to Alicia and me. We said farewell, and I watched as the flight attendants went out the cabin door followed by the purser.

In my mind Alicia would be next in line to exit the plane. I asked her, and she didn't seem to mind. I thanked her again, we said goodbye, and she took the few steps out through the cabin door and down the stair to relative freedom. (None of us is absolutely free as long as we have others who we care for and who care for us…)

I was now the last person leaving the plane. Why did that have such significance for me? I don't quite know, but to me it felt like this was my pay, and the only compensation I wanted or needed. I had actually stepped up and taken responsibility. I had been convinced that we were going to crash and die, but I had nevertheless accepted the responsibility to sit in the captain's seat, fully aware that in doing so, all fingers would initially point at me as the cause of the crash. I wanted to show, at least to myself, that I had earned the right to be the last person leaving. It was a gift I wanted to give to myself, and I felt an immense gratitude towards the purser who, by his courtesy, had awarded me this opportunity. At last, I had actually done something to be proud of. I didn't want to miss out on celebrating that. I felt almost like a real captain.

At the foot of the stair, I stopped. First, I looked up to the skies and gave thanks for the outcome. (God is not a vending machine which you use to put in a prayer, to later collect what you asked for, but this doesn't mean that you shouldn't express your gratitude whenever you realise that thanks are due.) Then I turned around and gave thanks to the plane. What a fantastic airplane! I noticed that the ground crew, or whoever they were standing on the runway, were watching me with surprise and questions in their faces: Who is this guy? What is he doing? I didn't explain or apologise for my behaviour. I just did what I thought appropriate in that situation to do.

I started walking towards the main terminal building of the airport, aiming for the welcoming sign of "Arrivals". I remember thinking: So, squawk code is it. Really? Not squeak code, not squeal code… Ha! Who knew?

Epilogue

The days following our arrival in Botswana were both intense and boring. My previous notion that we would not see each other after we left the plane, turned out to be correct. Those of us who were regarded as essential to the investigation were kept separated from each other by being kept in different hotels. The hotel where I stayed was very nice. It was a five-star hotel in the centre of the city with exquisite cuisine and excellent service. I didn't lack anything, except perhaps the freedom to leave the hotel and do whatever I wanted. There was a policeman in the corridor outside the room, who guarded my door (and me, presumably), and who also accompanied me to the interviews which took place at the police headquarters.

I did my best to give account for what had occurred on the plane, and tried to be as precise and truthful as I could. I also did my best to explain that the young hijacker, whom I shot and wounded, had played a minor part in this event and could not be regarded as someone who had been involved in the planning of the hijacking and possibly not even essential for its execution.

Of all the participants in the drama, only a few were deemed necessary or important for the investigation. Actually, very few. The flight attendants were free to leave after a day or two when they had given their statements to the police, and so was Alicia. The only persons who had to stay a bit longer were the purser and myself. Because of an administrative slip up from the side of the police we actually met unguarded for a couple of minutes at the police headquarters. We exchanged compliments and the little news we each had picked up thus far in the process. I also learned that the purser actually had a name. It consisted of very many letters in an unfortunate combination, making it impossible for me both to pronounce and to remember. Luckily his job title was easier in both regards.

At one point, a newspaper journalist showed up at the hotel asking for an interview with me. I declined. The reasons were several. First of all, the police had asked me not to discuss these matters with anyone during the ongoing investigation. Secondly, I had no wish to appear in any newspaper, neither in Botswana, nor anywhere else.

In the reception of the hotel, a couple of days later, I saw a picture of the plane on the first page of a national newspaper. I bought the paper, which luckily was in English. The article which belonged to said picture described the hijacking of a plane from Maputo with destination Windhoek. For reasons not entirely clear, since the investigation is still ongoing and the police is reluctant to disclose any details, the plane made a successful emergency landing at Maun International Airport. The miraculous landing was no doubt due to the skills and professional training of the excellent staff of the Botswanan Air Traffic Control, as well as an outstanding performance of the police, the medical staff, the ground crew and other personnel at Maun International Airport. The article didn't mention any of us who had actually been on the plane during the ordeal. I didn't mind. Nor did I mind the description given of the role the Botswanan authorities and officials had played. They had a huge part in the overall positive outcome, and we owed them a lot. All in all, I had no objection to the article. I'm just glad I wasn't in it.

After ten days I was free to leave. The police had received all the information I had to give, and they had compared it with information from other sources (aka the purser). They were therefore satisfied, and I was no longer forced to stay in my luxurious confinement. The hotel was, as I mentioned earlier, very nice, but exactly how fancy my temporary incarceration had been was made clear to me when I checked out; I had to pay for it. All of it. Room and meals and whatnot. That dug a hole in my savings account deep enough to make me begin to see the bottom.

Don't get me wrong. I do understand that the Botswanan government hadn't actually asked for a plane full of passengers, hijackers and dead people to end up on their soil. The cost for medical services, police and all of the judiciary system etc, etc, must have been substantial. I guess that they had other, more urgent financial obligations, than paying for the accommodation of unwanted guests. It's just that, if I had known that I were to pay for my own involuntary captivity, I would probably have preferred a somewhat cheaper accommodation…

However, thanks to the invention of the credit card, I was still able to make it home. A credit card is a device which makes it possible for people who don't have any money, to forget about this for a while. Credit cards are like alcohol in that way. They allow us to forget about the reality, which then in turn will become twice as bad, due to the consequences these means of escapism bring to said reality.

The actual court trial was set to take place two months later. I was fully aware of what I had made myself guilty of on the plane, which means that I was a bit apprehensive regarding what would or could happen in the trial. I have a pretty good idea of what would have happened to me and my part in the events, had this taken place in my own country; All of my actions would have been scrutinised, assessed and judged, and I would most likely have been prosecuted for having discharged a firearm, not only once, but twice. This according to the principle – "Could there have been another possible course of action?" (Coincidently, that is the question which haunts me every night.) Would that have resulted in any severe punishment for me? I don't know, but I eagerly awaited the outcome of the Botswanan trial. Since I was not even asked to attend as a witness, I anticipated the ruling, but nevertheless I wanted the court to announce the final ruling before I could leave that fear properly behind me.

As it turned out, the court took on a rather practical and simple (I refrain from using the word "simplistic") view of the matter. This meant that the court found the hijackers to be the perpetrators, and everyone else on the plane were regarded as victims. Subsequently, the captured and unharmed hijacker was sentenced to twenty years in prison and the wounded younger hijacker was sentenced to ten years in prison. No one else faced any charges whatsoever.

One interesting aspect of this entire ordeal was that no one was able to find out exactly what the hijackers tried to achieve, or where they wanted to go. What was their objective? The person who most likely could have answered that question was the leader of the gang, and he was dead. The captured and unharmed hijacker refused to answer any questions or give anything away, neither in the police interrogations, nor in the court hearing. When the third hijacker had recovered enough to be questioned, he denied knowing anything about the overall goal of the hijacking. He was only recruited as a general help, on a "need-to-know basis", and he claimed that he never actually "needed to know". This could very well be true. He was neither the boss, nor the administrative planner of the endeavour. He never struck me as anyone else than someone caught with his helping hand in a cookie jar where it never should have been.

I've had ample time since we landed to go through the events on the plane. I feel tremendous gratitude towards the people who stepped up; The Frenchman (or whatever nationality he was), the purser, Daniel, Alicia and others. Without them, we wouldn't have made it. But I also thought about the seemingly insignificant gesture I had made towards the young girl, sitting in the middle seat of the row next to me. If I hadn't swapped seats with her, I would never have had the opportunity to follow the Frenchman (or whatever nationality he was) out into the aisle. He could have been shot by the hijacker who stood in the front, and that would have been the end of it. None of the subsequent events would in that case have occurred, and everything would have been different. I guess that whenever you show someone kindness, you never fully know what that means to the other person, or indeed not even what effect it may have on yourself and your own life further down the road. Maybe what I'm trying to say is: "Never miss a chance to be kind to others. You don't always know the importance and consequence of what your act of kindness may bring to the other person, or to yourself."

I realised that everything happening during these events, and the outcome of it, all depended on a series of coincidences. But, isn't that what life is? A countless number of coincidences. And the outcome is ultimately depending on how we deal with them. What we encounter throughout our lives may or may not be the consequences of our own previous decisions, but in the end it's all about whether we take responsibility for ourselves and our lives, or not. Blaming our circumstances and blaming others doesn't lead us forward, it doesn't make us grow, it only makes us bitter and miserable.

Well at home I returned to the life I knew. To begin with, I must say that it felt rather good to be back in the familiar tranquillity of my home. My idea of possibly moving to Africa had been gradually abandoned. A life in Africa was perhaps not for me, after all. Although boring, there was something stable and predictable with my life in small-town Sweden. The absence of poisonous snakes, scorpions, spiders, lethal parasites, crocodiles and other dangerous animals, spoke loudly in favour of my not moving to Africa. To visit Africa had been a splendid and exciting adventure, but then again, it was probably not for me to permanently live there. One reason for making the trip in the first place, was to provide me with the basis for making a decision on where to live, or where not to live. But, in the end, "boring and familiar" seemed to me like a pleasant alternative to "exciting and potentially life-threatening" …

It's not that I hadn't noticed that my African excursion had changed me to some extent, it's just that it's somewhat difficult to put the finger on exactly what the changes were. In one way, we never change. The set of genes and the basic personality traits we are born with follow us until the day we die. On the other hand, every event, every experience, every person we encounter and every decision we make, changes us. If we are in a position to choose, and if we choose wisely – it may even change us for the better.

So, I continued my life as I was used to live it, and yet some changes I actually could recognise. One being; I didn't regret making the trip. Up until this point, my life had been filled with regrets. I've had regrets concerning practically everything, whether it being something I've said or something I've done. Now, I find myself accepting every decision I've made in the past, regardless of the outcome. I acknowledge that every decision, wise or stupid, every victory or defeat, every success or failure, has led me to the point where I am today. My mistakes and failures have all been essential parts in making me who I am. If I hadn't made all those mistakes in the past and come to learn from them, then I guess they would still lie ahead of me as disasters waiting to happen. Of course, I regret everything I've done which has hurt other people, but that's another story. That, I have to live with.

I still buy my eggs in cartons containing three rows of five, by the way, but I don't make a big deal out of it. I can actually accept the thought of eggs being packed in other types of cartons. It wasn't extremely important to me before either, but it's just that it's even less important now. I guess I've noticed and accepted that my perception and appreciation of things have changed.

Another thing is that I've become more convinced than ever, that it's important to not stop living until one is dead. This life can consist of anything one wants, whether it may be sitting in one's favourite couch and watching familiar sights, or making a trip to Machu Picchu for the first time.

So then, what am I supposed to do with my few remaining years? I was back, not only in my familiar home and surroundings, but also with the familiar question which was the origin of, and the basic reason for, my African adventure. One has to occupy oneself with something even if one is retired. It can't all be just a period of wait for the inevitable. I'm not quite ready to accept that.

I looked back at my life. Accounting – that was the life I chose. I don't regret it. It's an honourable profession. It paid the bills for my family and me, and I actually enjoyed working as an accountant.

But, maybe it's time to choose again, something new, something exciting, something a bit more challenging…

So, I started writing